THEY CALLED HIM MR. HORNE; THE ARAPAHO CALLED HIM GRAY WOLF

Elizabeth Simmons was the only one who dared speak.

"Bring back my girls, Mister Horne," she pleaded. "Please!"

Horne did not reply.

They watched him ride up the trail until he was small and dark and then he disappeared over the ridge, leaving them alone with their thoughts, the terrible suspicions that had already begun to fester like a swelling boil in their minds.

SOMEWHERE IN THE STORM, WORLDS WERE ABOUT TO COLLIDE

Tor books by Jory Sherman

Horne's Law
The Medicine Horn
Song of the Cheyenne
Winter of the Wolf

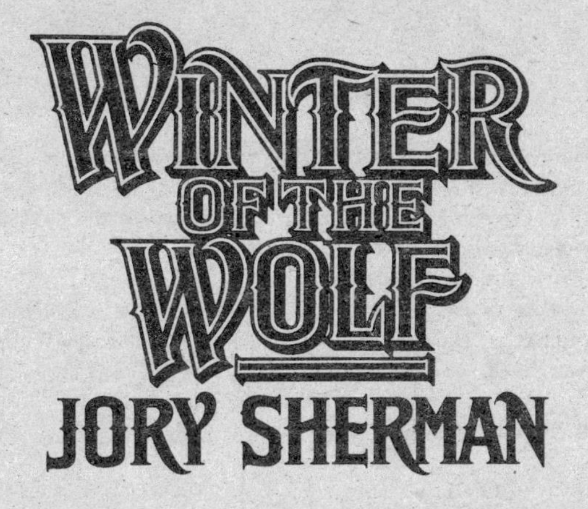

JORY SHERMAN

A TOM DOHERTY ASSOCIATES BOOK
NEW YORK

WINTER OF THE WOLF

Published by arrangement with Walker and Company

Cover art by Maren

A Tor Book
Published by Tom Doherty Associates, Inc.
175 Fifth Avenue
New York, N.Y. 10010

ISBN: 0-812-58871-1
Library of Congress Catalog Card Number: 87-10505

First Tor edition: May 1989

Printed in the United States of America

0 9 8 7 6 5 4 3 2

For Richard S. Wheeler, novelist, editor, friend.

The achieved West had given the United States something that no people had ever had before, an internal, domestic empire.

Bernard De Voto

WINTER
OF THE
WOLF

PROLOGUE

THE man on the Indian pony, a steeldust gray, picked his way over the rimrock, his eyes restless beads in movable sockets, the flesh at the corners squinched to block the blinding glint of weak sun on snow. The big Hawken .54, the brass patchbox dulled and mottled by weather and time, rested easy in his right hand, the barrel laid across the shoulder of the plain cowhide pommel, the stock balanced on the calf of his elkskin-clad leg. He was big, even in his oversized sheepskin-lined antelope coat, the sleeves and bottom fringed to draw rain from its surface. He wore a dark felt hat cut from a thick bolt, and five days of coal black beard. His features were flattened under high cheekbones that were divided in a symmetrical design by a nose that had been broken at least once at the bridge, giving it the angular shape of a hawk's beak.

Draped across the gray's rump, behind the flared cantle of his Denver saddle, a pair of fresh lion skins flapped with each rocking movement of the horse. A dark broom of hair, still green and uncured, torn from an Arapaho's scalp, hung from the saddlehorn by a tough strand of sinew. Two other scalplocks, long, silky, and rust red, tied at the stumps with water-blotched pink ribbons, dangled from the horn on the opposite side of the pommel.

The man held a thumb over the crosshatched hammer as he topped the rimrock, looked at the valley below. The rope, gathered up in his left hand with the reins, went slack, and a moment later, the spotted Indian pony behind him scrambled to the flat rocky spine of the ridge.

On the pony rode a young girl. Her hands, mittened in

ermine-lined deerskin coverings, clung tightly to the horn of the Santa Fe saddle as if she was afraid she would tumble down the opposite slope of the mountain. Her face was freckled with tiny dark circles the color of copper pennies. Her reddish hair was straight, the curls long since ironed out by rain and sweat and the rinsing waters of mountain streams. She was bundled in a woolen trade blanket and cap, her mouth slack and open, fixed as if frozen in a perpetual silent scream.

The man on the steeldust did not look back at her, but scanned the hard land he knew so well. The ridge was strewn with rock, ground down by the slide of ancient glacial ice. The ice, like a river, had once moved down this valley, following the real river's course; had moved slowly over this treacherous precipice, then broken up into deltas. The glacier had crushed and polished the bedrock as it flowed across the valley, capturing gigantic boulders and slowly grinding them to a smooth, flat finish, until some resembled the faceted conical shapes of diamonds.

Below this valley, he knew, the old glacier had paused in its melting retreat and dropped a load of debris. The rubble formed a moraine that dammed the valley, leaving behind a deep blue lake. After that, the trees grew and, over time, their stands became uniform.

The valley appeared to have been landscaped by a gardener. The tall ponderosa pines grew in open stands of trees that were all the same age. But no gardener had come through here and done this. Instead, the weather had a hand in these formations of uniform growth, starting the small fires that burned patches of trees, the first ones taking out the dead timber, consuming the litter of the forest floor. This burn-out left behind a seedbed of ashes, a perfect breeding place for new young trees.

Seeds from the pines drifted over the wasteland and germinated, taking root and thriving until the soil was again littered with the tinder of pine needles, fodder for the sparks generated by random strikes of lightning.

A stream ran through the valley, into the lake, and beaver had once made the floor marshy and lush so that now the alders, willows, birches and blue spruce grew in old ponds along the stream's meandering course.

He sniffed the air. It smelled musty and stale, tasted of moisture, of snow waiting to fall.

He looked again at the low clouds, leaden and bulging, pregnant with a swelling moistness that threatened to burst their bellies. The distant peaks, he saw, were blotted out, shrouded in a cloudmist where the fading light played with shadows.

His hat brim streaked his stark blue eyes with a ribbon of shade, eyes that squinted now against the dying yellow light of the sun. He clapped blunted spurs to his horse's flanks, reined the gelding toward a path he himself had worn down over the years. The horse gingerly stepped down the talus slope, hooves gripped the soil under the loose scrabble of rock, slid over patches of blackened snow, slick as pyrite. The slack jerked loose from the rope as it tautened in the man's hand and the sure-footed Indian pony followed the steeldust's lead.

The man brushed off some of the dried blood that had caked on his jacket. The blood was not his own.

The trail wound past the stunted pines, windbent mountain cedars, the twisted, writhing limbs of the chill-blasted junipers. Here, he could smell the far-off woodsmoke, and when he looked, he saw the faint curl of smoke above the tree line. He scanned the treetops again, saw another pillar of blue-gray smoke that broke up into wisps as it cleared the trees, caught a vagrant whiff of breeze that blew down from the peaks of the far dark mountains.

"Horne, please," the girl said. "I—I don't want to go back there. I—I can't."

"You hush up, Mary Lee," Jack Horne gruffed, his voice a velvet rasp. "You got to go back. Some things you just gotta face."

Mary Lee Simmons sniffled and broke into tears again. The sobs came unbidden, deep and wracking, as if something inside her was tearing her flesh apart, breaking her bones into pieces as if they were brittle sticks.

Horne's face hardened into a mask as the gelding raced the last few feet down the slope, cleared the brush and came to a stiff-legged halt as the Indian pony caught up. He said nothing, remembered that it had been more than three months since he had left Sky Valley. He had tracked the small band of Arapahos who had taken the three white girls one afternoon when the snow lay deep and mounded in drifts that were like the ghost graves of earlier pioneers in the long shadows of winter twilight.

CHAPTER 1

LOUIS SIMMONS watched the other men in the settlement ride out of the valley, single-file. He did not like to see them go all in a bunch like that, but the settlement needed meat and the snows had been early and high that winter of '52. The deer and elk had drifted down off the moraines to the lowlands, or, if they hadn't, they had been stranded in some pocket, died of cold and starvation. He had seen that happen, too, over the years. Winter kill.

He pulled at his beard and bushy moustache that bent like a black horseshoe over his mouth, drew a macintoshed sleeve across his leaky nose. Louis had once been a lean man, but had developed a paunch the past few years. He could not ride for long periods anymore, nor even sit in one place without his knees stiffening up. He was nearing the half-century mark, and there was little hair left on his head, just a pair of fringes along the sides, and these turning gray with the dusting of each long winter in the high country.

"They go, Louis?" called his wife, Elizabeth. Her voice was muffled behind the chinked log cabin that held the ground on a knoll some fifty yards from McGongile's Trapper's Post.

"Yes, dear," he said, looking at the berms thrown up when he and Caleb had shoveled a path between Louis' cabin and the trading post. Two months of snowfall lay piled here and there, and snowshoe tracks were frozen hard on trails leading to the other cabins in the valley.

The post was a joke to some, but not to Louis Simmons. It was no longer a storehouse for furs, but a meeting place for the settlement folk, a place to sit by the potbellied stove and talk of old times with a drink of whiskey or rum in your hand. Caleb McGonigle had not gone with the hunters, either. He was older than Louis by some eight or ten years, and he had been one of the first to settle in Sky Valley.

Like most of the others, Caleb was Scotch-Irish, one of those northern Irish refugees that no country wanted for a citizen. But he was a good sort, had made his way in the world like Joe Walker and so many others who had come west to live without being persecuted.

Simmons too, had his reasons for settling here with these tight-mouthed, almost sullen people, who were clannish to an almost unbearable degree. Here, in this valley of stately lodgepole pine, blue and Engelmann spruce, fir and aspen, he had found a new homeland for his wife and three daughters, a sovereign state where every man was a king. The others had come in the early forties, looking for fur, the lucky gold strike, the fortune hidden in the ageless mountains.

But there was not much gold and the fur trade died out fast after '39, yet still the people hung on. Instead of monetary wealth, they found instead a world full of haunting beauty and unexpected danger. They listened in the long silence of winter to the howl of the wolf, heard the bugling of an elk in a distant meadow sounding like the lonesome call of the hunter's horn. And they didn't care when the beaver trade died out and the gold pans ran thin. They stayed on, stubborn as the lichen clinging to the bald faces of granite mountain peaks above timberline. They brought in seed and cattle and mules and oxen; they bought trade goods cheap and sold them dear in the scattered mountain settlements.

They stayed on, selling their woven blankets, linens and pottery in Walden and Laramie and Cheyenne. French and German settlers came, men who made rifles and plowshares and harness with their hands, who settled in and put down strong roots, stubborn as the land. The game was plentiful, the streams teeming with fish, and the sky so blue and perfect and private they could think of no better place on earth to live.

But another man was here before them, one who was laconic and raised horses, lived alone, hunted alone beyond the high rim that ringed the lush valley. No one knew much about him and few had even talked to him face to face. His name was Jackson Horne, and he rarely came down to McGonigle's. They all wondered about him as they raised their families, married among themselves. The settlement grew and prospered because there was plenty of water, and no law and they were free.

Yet some of them—Louis and Caleb and Chollie Winder, Bill MacPherson, Faron MacGregor, for a few—admitted that they often felt like intruders, because Horne had been there before them, was still there now. He had never said a word against them, however, nor had he claimed any land beyond what he needed for his horses and cabin. But, when some had tried to befriend him, he had cut them off short, saying they had best tend to their lives, leave him to his.

"Mister Simmons?"

Louis, jarred away from his thoughts, snapped his head at the sound of the high-pitched voice.

Little Angus MacPherson stood a few feet away, twirling a stick in his hand. Ah, they still called him Little Angus, Simmons thought, but the boy was nigh fourteen years of age, though puny. He had some kind of lung disease that made him choke and gasp for air in the nightchill, and Elizabeth thought it stunted his growth. He was shorter than most boys his age, and a heap thinner. Faron MacGregor's wife, Annis, who taught the children at the summer arbor school, said the boy was smart enough, but had no strength. When he played with the other children, he ran out of breath and his face would turn blue as the columbines.

"Dear me," she said, often enough to be irritating, "the poor boy is so thin, when he turns sideways I'm bound to mark him absent from his learning class."

No one laughed at that anymore. The boy was thin; and even in summer, his ribs showed bony through his skin.

"What is it, Angus?"

"Uh, I was wondering if Mary Lee could come out and play snowballs with me?"

The boy fidgeted, poked the stick down into the snow and roiled the earth up with little flicks of his wrist. He had the strawberry hair that was all cowlick; it grew in all directions, and big bright eyes that were brown as coffee beans. He wore a woolen sweater his mother, Wilma, had spun for him on her loom, and gray duck pants that bulged from the layers of long underwear underneath.

"Now, boy, you know Mary Lee's too old for you. Why, she's of marryin' age, almost. Don't think she'd be a-playin' snowballs with you."

"There isn't anyone else to play with," Angus said stubbornly.

"Well, I'll talk to her. You just find yourself something to do, meantime."

Angus' face clouded up and he hurled the stick through the air, watching it twirl in flight until it plunged into a mound of snow and the floured earth swallowed it up. He ran behind the Simmons cabin and started building a snowman.

Caleb walked out onto the porch of the cabin, shook out a bear rug. It was a small rug, made from a cub's hide, and it looked motheaten, but was not. This was the rug he kept under his rocking chair in the back where he lived. He smoked a pipe and always spilled hot ashes into the fur, so that there were bare swatches where the pelt had been burned away.

"Men all gone?" he asked, in that peculiar Scotch-Irish twang that made the words sound like part of a song.

Louis nodded.

"Don't like it much, them going off like that, all of a bunch."

"We can take care of things, Lou. I've some whiskey coming prime in the barrel. Come tonight and we'll taste the creature, just you and I."

Simmons laughed, even though he did not want to laugh. He was concerned, but McGonigle wasn't. He never was. Of them all, he had prospered best, perhaps, because he stored the staples, made the whiskey in iron pots and copper tubing, and kept his methods a secret. In years past, his wagons rolled when no others did and he brought goods to the valley that no one else had sense enough to go after and bargain for in Laramie or Cherry Creek.

McGonigle shook the rug again and flotsam sprinkled on the white snow like pepper on a mashed potato.

"Just hope they make meat this trip," said Lou.

"Ah, they will, Lou, if they go far enough. Maybe to the fort, though it be a long ride and a cheerless one on the way back."

Fort Collins was a steep ride down the Cache de la Poudre Canyon, all downhill. If the men had to go onto the plains, they could be gone a month or more if the snows were heavy. Lou didn't want to think about that. He didn't feel good about the men being gone at all.

"They won't go that far," said Lou. "Berle said they'd be back tomorrow."

Berle Campbell had organized the hunting party. He said they would either find game down on the flat where the moraine had blocked out a valley protected on all sides by high mountains, or they would not find game at all. They had taken just enough food to last them a day.

"And they will, Lou, they will," said Caleb. He rolled up the small bear rug and drew his pipe out of a trouser pocket. He filled it with rich dark tobacco that smelled like apples, struck a sulphur match on the porch rail, attached the flame to the center of the briar's bowl. "'Tis not a far ride and sure they'll scare up a stag or two out of the willows along the river. I can taste the meat now, all juicy and prime, like the coon we used to eat back in the Creek Nation when I was but a tad."

Lou walked over to the porch, caught a glimpse of Little Angus rolling a chunk of snow into a ball as if it was a carpet.

The snow was wet from the sun's heat, and the air warm enough to melt it some. For a moment he was blinded by the reflection off the pearly surface and he blinked at the searing light.

Caleb leaned against a stripped pine post, puffed on his briar pipe, let the smoke snake into his nostrils as his lungs swelled, billowed under his faded linsey-woolsey shirt that had once been dyed blue, was now a pale sand color.

Louis sat on a step, flexed his knees, heard them crack like stepped-on twigs. Sometimes he thought the kneecaps would just break open and he would be a cripple the rest of his life. It was hell on a man, growing old. Just when he was getting to like life, his body was turning on him.

He heard a leather hinge creak, saw his daughter Mary Lee dash out into the snow. She was the youngest of his three daughters, nigh eighteen and his favorite. With her freckly face and soft white skin, she was the image of Elizabeth when he had met her. Sally May was the next eldest, at twenty, and Betsy June had just turned twenty-two. He was fond of all of them, and hoped Betsy June would marry soon. There was a young man courting her, but he lived in Walden and would not be seen again until spring.

Mary Lee circled the cabin, her skirt flying under the two-point capote she wore over it. Her laughter, as she joined Little Angus in play, floated on the air like streamers of sparkling ribbons.

"You've a fine family, Louis," said Caleb.

"Umm." Caleb's wife had died of pneumonia two years before. They had no children. Edith had been barren, taken on fat over the years. Elizabeth said if she had been thinner she would have survived the pneumonia. That was little comfort to Caleb, who loved her dearly. Edith used to make dresses for all the women, had been quite imaginative.

"I'll have some strong tea after a while," said Caleb, "the last of the sassafras 'till spring."

"I'll drink a cup with you."

"Bring Elizabeth, too."

"She was going to go to the Campbell cabin, look in on Colleen."

"She dearly loved sassafras tea," mused Caleb, and Louis knew the man was still pining for his woman.

"Maybe she can bide a wee 'fore she visits Missus Campbell."

Both men stiffened as they heard a shriek from behind Louis' cabin. Louis tried to stand up, but his right knee locked on him, and he nearly fell. Caleb's mouth dropped open as the cabin filled with shouts, the shrill screams of the women.

"What. . .?" Louis started to say.

A moment later, Mary Lee ran past the corner of the cabin, followed by Little Angus.

"Pa," she yelled, "somebody's coming. Wild Indians."

"Wild Indians," echoed Angus.

McGonigle went to the edge of the porch, looked up toward the northeastern rim of the surrounding range of mountains.

The Simmons cabin emptied as Elizabeth, Betsy June and Sally May ran outside, headed toward McGonigle's. Their faces were drawn and blanched with fear.

"Lou. . ." Elizabeth's voice quavered.

She was a sturdy woman, thin, bony, with a hooked nose, a large brown mole sprouting next to it. Her graying hair was swept back from her wide, flat forehead, combed into a bird's nest bun in back, tied with a faded ribbon. Her printed floral dress was drab, gray from many washings, threadworn in places. Her arms jutted thin and bony from three-quarter cotton sleeves. Her lips were finely etched, drawn together tightly against carrious teeth.

Louis heard his kneecap make a loud crack as he got to his feet. He stepped toward his daughters, his wife, waded through them for a better view of the Indians.

"Hush," he told the women, who started chattering hysterically all at once. "Don't get excited. Could be friendly. Just lost."

"Pa, I'm scared," said Mary Lee, and her sisters caught her up in their arms, brought her into the huddle with their mother. Little Angus stood to one side, looking over his shoulder, frozen with fright.

"Caleb? What do you make of it?" Louis saw them, then, a wavering line of riders, dark against the snow, coming their way.

"Better get the women inside, load up your Harper's Ferry rifle, Louis."

Louis swallowed hard, could not speak for a moment. He looked at his wife's eyes, saw the terror there. He drew in a breath, gathered strength from her anxiety somehow.

"Elizabeth, I want you to walk, don't run, to the cabin, you and the girls. Go inside and latch it, drop the crossbar. You set my rifle by the door."

"What are you going to do, Pa?" asked Betsy June, the eldest. Her hair was an autumn flame against her alabaster skin.

"Maybe they just want to trade. Now, go on, but don't show that you're afraid.'"

"They ain't Utes," said Caleb, eyes still fixed on the slow-moving procession. "Wearing feathers. All bundled up in buffalo robes, so I can't rightly see them fair."

Louis shooed his wife and daughters toward the cabin, noticed Angus still standing there.

"Angus, you'd best go on home, tell your ma to batten down."

Angus looked at Simmons in confusion. His lower lip was trembling.

"Go on," urged Louis. "Caleb and I will talk to these redskins."

Angus pretended to leave, but he did not go very far. He hid behind a spruce, squatting under the lower branches so that he could watch McGonigle's without being seen.

"Caleb?" said Louis. "There's a dozen at least."

"A dozen, yes. Don't seem to be in no froth. Ain't hurryin' none at all."

The Indians came on, their silhouettes growing larger. A spotted pony, riderless, frisky in the chill air, trotted out of the line, and the Indian reined the animal back to its former position.

Louis' throat went dry as sand. Caleb spilled hot ashes from his pipe onto his leg, paid them no attention, though they must have scorched his flesh.

"Well, I'll be a son of a buck," breathed Caleb.

"What?"

"Them are Arapahos for certain sure, Louis. Seen some before, but none since we run the Utes out."

"Arapahos? What are they doing here? Hunting?"

Caleb turned toward Simmons, looked him in the eyes.

"No, that's no hunting party, Louis. Look close at their faces. They're painted like masks of the devil himself, painted for war."

Simmons felt his knees turn liquid, and something knotted in his belly, made his dry throat burn with bile. He fought the vomitus down, looked at his small log cabin.

His lips moved soundlessly as he tried to speak.

The Arapahos rode closer, their ponies tramping the snow, snorting jets of steam through rubbery nostrils.

For a long time that was the only sound, those hoofs breaking through the snowcrust, and it kept getting louder and louder, until it was like the sound of a terrible avalanche slowly gathering speed as it slips down the side of a mountain, destroying everything in its path.

CHAPTER 2

THE Arapaho came on, painted and buckskinned underneath winter coats of fox and beaver, buffalo and antelope, riding slow, half-frozen, gaunt from hunger, their eyes bright with the madness of starvation. The leader, a thin bony buck of little more than twenty-five winters, held the others in line behind him with gutteral whispers. McGonigle's dogs barked, and Arapaho eyes glittered like agates in a sunstruck pool.

Besides the pinto, there were two other riderless horses with the Arapaho. These, too, were painted for battle, but their owners lay dead in high snows, pierced by Ute arrows, smashed to pieces by Ute warclubs. The Arapaho had lost two mounts, taken no horses and no women, and they had seen no game in days of riding south from the high camp of the Ute. They had lived on pine bark and roots for a moon, and were now chewing on leather breechclouts as their stomachs knotted in pain.

The paint on their faces was cracked and smeared, fading from the effects of wind and blown snow, but the Arapaho still looked fearsome to McGonigle as they rode single file toward his trading post.

"Louis, quit whimperin'," breathed Caleb.

"Gawd, Caleb, what do they want?"

"Maybe only some whiskey. You best take holt of yourself."

"Shoot them, Caleb," Simmons croaked, but McGonigle did not hear him. His dogs began to bark more loudly and ran toward the Arapaho before he could stop them. There were three of them, half-wild mongrels that had not been fed much this early winter, their coats thick over bony skeletons.

McGonigle pursed his lips to whistle, but no sound came out. The dogs ran at the horses, their barks turning to yaps, changing pitch. Their paws kicked up snow, turned it to a thick mist, blotting out their gaunt bodies as they dove for fetlocks, snapped at unshod hooves. The Indian ponies arched their necks, slid lips back over large sharp teeth.

A pair of braves in the middle of the line of horses slid from their mounts, silent as wraiths, shadows hitting the snow. The dogs did not see them until it was too late. The braves waded into the small pack, wielding stone war clubs. Caleb thought he could hear the faint rush of air from the hawk feathers attached to the shafts of the clubs, but he could not be sure. His heart hammered in his ears, thumping like the hooves of the Indian horses as they broke from formation in panicked flight from the sharp, nipping fangs of the dogs.

"No!" Caleb breathed, but his voice carried no farther than the steam spewing from his dry mouth.

One of the braves strode close to a reddish-brown dog, raised his club over his head and struck downward before the dog could leap out of the way. The clubhead wiped a blurred path through the air, smacked into the dog's skull with a sickening crunch.

Louis Simmons gasped, sucked air that would not come into his lungs. His eyes blurred with a sudden sting from unbidden tears. Caleb's mouth dropped open as the dog crumpled into the snow, blood spurting from its head, splashing crimson as if someone had hurled a bucket of paint into the snow.

The other brave brought his club down hard on another dog's back. There was a snapping sound, like a branch breaking under the weight of snow and the dog yelped in pain, tried to bite its tail. It spun in circles, dragging its useless hindquarters through the snow. Both braves ran after the remaining dog. Startled, it had leaped back, away from the men on foot, and, off balance, scrambled to get its feet under him. The two braves came at it from both sides, cutting it off. One brave slammed the club into the dog's ribs. The dog stumbled, rolled over and the second brave clubbed it on the nose. The animal tried to stand up, but both men rained blows off its head, drawing blood with every smash of stone. The dog whimpered, screamed, tried to swing its head out of the way, but the hard rocks of the clubs mangled its features, knocked out teeth, hammered an eye to jelly, beat its head bloody until it could rise no more.

The second dog continued to whine and scream, floundered in endless circles. The second brave clambered over to it and lifted his club with both hands. He drove it down hard, shattering the dog's skull, blasting splinters of bone into the brain. The dog went silent, slumped to its death, its tongue lolling purple from its slack mouth, its eyes glazed with the frosty sheen of death.

The dog-killers stood there, sweating in their heavy robes, breathing out heavy plumes of misty air as the other braves dismounted, drew their knives.

McGonigle turned away, knowing what the Arapaho would do. Louis Simmons staggered to his cabin, leaned against the porch.

"Don't look," he called, his voice hoarse with fear. "Elizabeth, don't let the girls see this."

Elizabeth Simmons, who was huddled with the three girls in the back of the house could not restrain her daughters from craning their necks to see out the back window. Mary Lee, the bravest, stood up straight and looked at the Indians openmouthed.

"They killed Mr. McGonigle's dogs," she whispered. "They're goin' to skin 'em."

"Hush," said her mother, who cowered in the corner, covering her face with her hands. "Don't look at them.

Maybe they'll go away." The tears welled up in her eyes, and she felt ashamed of her fear.

But the Arapaho did not go away. Three of the braves skinned the dogs, but did not gut them. Their voices, speaking in their own tongue, carried on the wind. Mary Lee wondered what they were saying.

"Make fire," said Iron Knife.

"Eat raw," argued Crow Caller.

The leader, who was called Red Hawk, decided the issue.

"Make fire," he said laconically, as he gestured toward two other braves. "We go. Talk trader."

Caleb McGonigle saw the three warriors striding his way, and he walked into the trading post. Dazed, the images of the dog killing still flashing unbidden in his mind, he looked for a weapon. He picked up a trade musket, checked the pan. There was no powder under the frizzen. He rummaged behind the counter for a flask, patch and ball. A few feet away stood a fully loaded .58 caliber Pennsylvania rifle, primed, ready to shoot.

Caleb spilled powder when he shook the brass flask and dropped the rifle. The sound made him jump and he did not pick up the rifle. He threw the powder flask on the counter and went to the door. He was still quivering inside and his hands shook so that he drove them into his pockets, out of sight.

A fear built up inside him. He looked at the rifle on the floor and the cold realization struck him that he might die. There was something about those Arapaho coming into the valley that was not right. They wore the paint and they had killed his dogs.

The dogs. He thought about them now and cringed inwardly. In his mind's eye, he saw them go down again under the clubs, saw their blood fleck the snow. Saw their lifeless bodies lifted up in triumph by a pack of savages.

Caleb walked outside, dreading what he would see, but

hoping the Indians had left. Maybe that was all they wanted. He knew they liked dog meat. He shuddered, thinking about it. But maybe they would go away.

"Louis," he said. "Have they. . .?" He saw Simmons hanging onto the corner post of the porch, his face contorted, his mouth twisted out of shape, his hair damp with sweat. Then, he saw the three braves breaking through the snow's crust on moccasined feet, coming toward him. The one in front wore a pair of hawk's feathers behind his ear and he carried a metal warclub, a hatchet set in wood that was studded with brass tacks, had symbols painted on it. The other two carried strung bows and their quivers bristled with feathered arrows.

"Caleb, they're skinning out the dogs," blubbered Simmons, who seemed permanently affixed to the porch post.

McGonigle saw that this was so. The braves jerked the bodies free of hides, like giant skinned squirrels, and draped them over their saddles. They threw the hides away like rags.

Two of the braves raided the woodpile in back of the trading post. Another cleared a spot for a fire. Caleb watched them, without counting them, but there were seven warriors in all. They looked like many more than that, and he could hear their strangely high-pitched and gutteral voices, the sing-song words seeming to slide out of throats and over teeth like scaly-skinned lizards. For these moments, time seemed to slow down for the trader, because he was seeing only bits and pieces of horror, of movement, and he seemed transfixed there at the side of his porch as if he was dreaming it all. And, too, it was as if he had seen it all before, each Indian moving in just these same ways.

Caleb shivered again and he knew it was not from the cold.

"Where young men?" asked the leader, his voice strong and deep, his accent thick as a buffalo tongue. He waved his battle ax at the clearing beyond the trading post. Caleb swallowed, felt his eyes bug out of their sockets like grapes squeezed through a funnel spout.

"Go away," he croaked, pulling his hands from his pockets. "Take the dogs and go away." He heard the scrape of flint on steel, saw the sparks fly into the shaved edges of the wood. One brave knelt down and blew on the tinder until the flame caught and the fire lapped at the dry wood, raced up the shavings.

"Where young men?" repeated the Indian as he stopped in his tracks.

"Hunting," croaked Simmons and Caleb pierced him with a look. He wanted to strangle Louis at that moment.

The Arapaho laughed and it was a chilling sound to hear. Caleb squinted and waved his hands again.

"You go. Now," he said, and there was no force to his words, but only a pleading undercurrent, a thinly disguised fear in his tone.

"Whiskey," said one of the other braves, and the other man laughed, made a sign with his hands of drinking from the burning cup.

"No whiskey," said Caleb weakly. "Bad for Injun."

There had been other Indians come to the valley over the years. Not like these. Once, some Utes had come up from the south, but they were shy, wary, and like children. They had wanted whiskey, too, and he had made them back down. But the other men were there then, and the Utes had gone away, sullen but cowed, and they had not come back although the men stayed on guard for weeks after that.

As if to wipe out the memory, a sudden wind gusted, kicked up snow behind the Arapaho, swirled it upward into the sun until the Indians disappeared in a miniature white blizzard, appearing only as shadows, like wavy images in a smeared window pane. The sunlight caught the motes, made them sparkle until Caleb saw only the dazzling, blinding light. He rubbed his eyes, wondered if he was losing his mind. Perhaps, he reasoned quickly, none of this was real. His thoughts clawed at the possibility that everything he had seen was only an hallucination, a crazy daydream that had never really happened. But the wind died, and he saw the Indians again, and his heart died with the wind, beat faintly in his chest. The windblown snow blew against his face and turned wet as it melted against his flesh. He knew then that he was surely going to die and that there was nothing he could do to stop it from happening.

Crow Caller whispered to Red Hawk: "The white man is afraid of you."

"It is so," said the leader.

"Maybe you should kill him," said Iron Knife. "There are only these two white men here. Both are swallowing the fear balls in their throats."

Red Hawk grunted. This old white man in front of him looked as if he was going to sing his death song. His eyes had the look of a man ready to take the star path to the sky home of his ancestors. The other white man was also crazy with fear, holding onto the tree of the porch like a wounded bear. This disgusted Red Hawk, made him angry.

"Why you no give Injun whiskey?" he asked, struggling with the white man's words. "We want whiskey. Much cold. Much hunger." Red Hawk crossed his arms and held his upper arms, then rubbed his belly.

Caleb blinked stupidly, licked his dry lips. It was almost as if he was locked onto a course from which he could not waver. He thought about giving the Indians whiskey, but only for a brief moment. He well knew what it would do to them. Especially in their present condition.

His pipe had gone cold and he realized he had bitten the stem nearly in two as he sucked in cold, ashy air.

"No, by God," he said.

Simmons heard Caleb and turned to look at the man. It was then that he saw little Angus McPherson squatting under the spruce tree, wide-eyed as a barn owl.

"Angus," he said, coming to his senses, "you best get on

home. Quick." Louis stood up, pushed away from the roof support. "Caleb, I'll get my rifle, back you."

He edged around the porch, stepped over the path's berm. He felt better now that he had made a decision. If Caleb could stand up to those redskins, so could he. Louis would say later that is was seeing the boy what brung him out of the fear-grip, made him think straight. Knowing the women were inside the cabin, scared, depending on him, too, made him forget about his own hide. There was some things more important, he reasoned.

"Louis, you step careful. . ." Caleb took the pipe from his mouth, stuck it in his pocket without shaking out the dead ashes.

Those were his last words.

Crow Caller whooped and charged Caleb McGonigle. He struck the man in the face with his warclub. Blood squirted down Caleb's neck and splashed on the front of his woolen shirt. The stone club sounded like a hammer splitting a melon. Caleb's legs bent inward, and he went down in one collapsing motion.

"Ahhhh," he screamed in agony, as he twisted on the snow.

Crow Caller brought the club down again, driving Caleb's head into the snow. The skull cracked like an eggshell, blood spurting from an artery until his heart stopped beating, staining the snow around his crushed head.

Crow Caller stood over the dead man, panting. He looked up at Red Hawk. Red Hawk stood impassive, silent. Angrily, Crow Caller dropped his club and drew his knife. He reached down, grabbed Caleb by the hair and jerked his smashed head out of the snow. He bent down and slashed both sides of the broken nose, then slammed the head down hard. Red Hawk grunted in approval.

Crow Caller reached down, picked up his club. He then slid a hand inside Caleb's jacket pocket, pulled out his pipe. He held it high for the others to see, then stuck it in his mouth. He grinned foolishly, and the other braves whooped a cry of victory. The smell of roasting dog wafted on the air. The men had cut the dogs in half, skewered them on lances.

"Elizabeth," croaked Louis. "Open the door, quick. Let me in."

Simmons clambered across the porch, began hammering on the door with his fists.

"Louis—I'm afraid!"

"Damnit, woman, open this door."

He heard the bar scrape against wood. The door opened a crack and Louis pushed his way inside. He snatched up his Lancaster musket, lifted the small powder horn off the nail in the cabin wall. Elizabeth craned to see outside. The girls came running into the front room, their faces chalky from fear.

"Father, we saw them. We saw the Indians." Sally May seemed mesmerized by the experience. Her sisters clustered close to her, watched as Louis fumbled with the powder horn, trying to take the peg out with his teeth. Fine black powder spilled on the floor as he shook it over the pan.

"What are you going to do, Louis?" asked Elizabeth, struggling for a calmness that was not there. Her pale blue eyes were rimmed with red where she had rubbed away the tears.

"They kilt Caleb, Elizabeth. They took his damned pipe."

It was a foolish thing to say and Elizabeth blinked in bewilderment.

"What?" she said, as he slammed the frizzen down over the pan, cocked the rifle.

Louis turned, started out the door.

"Oh," he exclaimed as he saw the Indian crouching at the edge of the porch.

Crow Caller made no sound as he threw the club at Louis' head. The stone struck Simmons in the stomach, knocking the wind from his chest. He doubled up in pain. Crow Caller climbed onto the porch, scrambled toward the stricken white man.

The Indian deftly scooped up his war club and straddled Simmons. Elizabeth choked back a scream as Crow Caller swung the club in a short, vicious arc. He brained Simmons, who fell sideways, unconscious.

Elizabeth screamed, dashed out the door. Terrified, she bounded from the porch and kept running as the Arapaho looked at her in surprise. Crow Caller, caught in a half-crouch, stared at the fleeing white woman who seemed to fly over the snow like a giant bird. He chuckled, stood up. He picked up the long-barreled Lancaster, turned it over in his hands.

"Get away from here," said Mary Lee Simmons defiantly.

Crow Caller turned, saw the three white girls standing in the doorway, their mouths pinched up in anger, their eyes smouldering slits. He looked at their faces and then at their luxuriant tresses.

He cackled to himself and stalked toward them as Mary Lee frantically lashed out with her hand to close the door. Betsy June Simmons screamed, which frightened her two sisters so that they began shrieking at the top end of their voices.

They were still screaming as Crow Caller pushed the closing door back open, hurling Mary Lee to the floor. Their cries brought the other Arapaho running. They pushed into the Simmons house behind Crow Caller. Mary Lee struggled to her feet, started to run toward the back of the cabin. She collided with her sisters and they all went down in a tangled heap.

They looked up, saw the hideous, painted faces of seven Arapaho warriors.

"Mother of God," gasped Sally May Simmons, "they're going to kill us dead."

CHAPTER 3

LITTLE Angus McPherson wondered what was wrong with Mrs. Simmons. She ran toward him but didn't even see him. Her eyes were fixed in their sockets, made her look strange. She didn't say anything, either. She must be plumb scared out of her wits to do that, he thought. He squatted there under the spruce tree and waved to her, but she ran right on past him, toward the Newcastle cabin which was a long way from the trading post.

He was scared at first, too. He had seen what the bad Indian had done to Mr. McGonigle and to Mr. Simmons. Both of them were asleep, but Mr. McGonigle was smashed like those dogs of his. That had been scary, especially when they skinned them out, began cooking them. When the girls had started screaming he had wanted to go and get Mary Lee to come and play with him, maybe go down to the creek and break off some ice to eat. He sure didn't want to build a snowman up here with all those mean Indians about.

He saw the Indians run up to Mr. and Mrs. Simmons' cabin and go inside. The girls made a powerful lot of noise with their screaming and then they stopped and it was real quiet for a long time. Angus wondered why it was so quiet all of a sudden.

Then he heard funny noises, and he crept out from under the spruce tree and sneaked up to look through the door. It was hard to breathe, he was so scared, and his heart made a noise in his ears like the hoofbeats of running deer. He peeked through the open front door and saw some Indian arms and parts of their leggings and breeches. He heard a lot of funny sounds and thought he heard Sally May call out for her father.

He saw Betsy June once, and she didn't have any of her clothes on and then he didn't see her anymore because one of the Indians jumped on her and they were wrestling like he and Gary Winder did sometimes—only he and Gary had their clothes on. He didn't like to look in there anymore, so he went around to look at the dogs, see what the Indians had done to them. He saw them, but they were all cut up and burned and still cooking. He didn't like the smell. It made him sick. He walked over to Mr. McGonigle and when he saw his face, Angus vomited in the snow.

His stomach hurt and he went back out to the spruce tree and squatted there until the sickness passed. He wanted to cry, but he started building a snow fort to take his mind off the bad things. He built a little wall between him and the cabin so the Indians wouldn't see him. He would pretend he had a rifle and could shoot every one of them.

Two of the Indians came out of the Simmons cabin and peed before they went into the trading post. Angus heard them knock things over inside and make a lot of noise. They came out carrying whiskey jugs and went back into the Simmons cabin. Then, a couple more Indians came out of the cabin carrying jugs and they went over to the fire and cut off some dog meat. They carried some of it back to the cabin, eating as they walked. Angus felt sick again and he built the fort a little higher, packing the snow hard with his fur-lined mittens, packing it down good and thick.

The Indians went in and out of the cabin, in and out of Mr. McGonigle's trading post, and one of them fell in the snow and laughed when he got up. He walked like Faron MacGregor sometimes did when he drank too much whiskey with Jacques Berthoud, the Frenchman. Angus saw that the Indians' faces were puffy and red and they didn't have their coats on anymore so he could see their loincloths and their butts. They peed on the porch and over against the trading post, and some of them squatted and grunted, rubbed their butts in the snow like a scooching dog.

He wondered when the girls would come out and play. He wanted to show them his fort. He had a front and two sides now, and he was going to build it even higher, maybe pour some water on it so that it would freeze. He started to get cold, but he didn't know where to go. Gary Winder had gone with his father, Chollie, to hunt and there was nobody to play with. He didn't want to go to the Newcastle cabin, either. If Mrs. Simmons was there, she would just look crazy like she did and maybe Mrs. Newcastle would ask a lot of questions like she always did.

The Indians kept coming and going, eating the dogs, throwing the bones out onto the porch of the Simmons cabin. Mr. Simmons hadn't moved and Angus thought he must be asleep. He didn't want to say "dead," but that's what Mr. McGonigle was and probably Mr. Simmons, too, and he hoped the Indians didn't cook them and eat them like they did Mr. McGonigle's dogs.

Angus thought about going home, but nobody was there. His father had gone hunting with the others and his mother was quilting with Mrs. Campbell. It was too lonesome at home and besides, he would have a lot to tell Gary Winder when he got back from hunting. About the Indians, and the dogs and Mr. McGonigle, Mr. Simmons, how Mrs. Simmons had run off scared crazy and he would show Gary his fort and tell him about the funny things he saw inside the Simmons cabin. He had a whole lot to tell his friend when he got back.

Some of the Indians went into the trading post again, and then some others caught up their ponies and they carried out sacks of tinkling bottles and sugar, and tins of coffee and meat, tied them to their saddles. They took some of Mr. McGonigle's blankets, too, and then some of the Indians brought the Simmons girls outside and they had clothes on, coats and scarves, too. Angus thought the girls looked odd, because their faces were bruised and looked like they had been crying.

Angus stood up behind his snow fort and saw that the Indians were taking the girls away. They put them on ponies and pulled their hair until they cried out. Angus got mad and he stepped out of his fort and ran over to an Indian who was kicking Mary Lee.

"Stop doing that," he said. "Mary Lee, don't go with them. I want you to see my fort."

Mary Lee looked at him with smokey sad eyes and she was crying, sobbing to herself, shaking her head. The other two girls did not look at him, but sat hunched over on their ponies, trembling all over as if they were shivering from the cold.

Seven Stars pointed to the boy and said something to Red Hawk. Wood Jumper grabbed the Lancaster rifle from Crow Caller and walked up to Angus, clubbed him with the butt. Angus cried out and crumpled to the snow. Wood Jumper poured some powder into the pan, closed the frizzen and took aim at the boy's chest.

"No, please don't shoot Angus," screamed Mary Lee, but Wood Jumper shot anyway.

There was a snap, a puff of smoke, a sound like a cough, then a big noise as the powder exploded. White smoke shrouded Wood Jumper and a white wreath of smoke blew from the muzzle toward the boy. Angus twitched as the ball smashed into his chest and mangled his little heart as the lead ripped through it and blew a big hole in his back dusting the snow with a spray of brilliant red blood.

Mary Lee sobbed and Diving Eagle rode up to her and slapped her mouth, spoke to her in Arapaho.

Sally and Betsy looked at Angus with dead, cold eyes. Their faces glistened with purple splotches and their lips were cracked and bleeding. One of Sally's eyes was puffed and closed, but she could see Angus' legs twitching and when the smoke cleared, she saw the black hole in his coat, the blood on the snow.

Wood Jumper grunted his approval and threw the empty rifle at Crow Caller.

"Let us go," said Red Hawk, mounting his horse. The others weaved as they walked to their horses, and their breaths reeked of whiskey. Gray Elk clutched a whiskey jug in his hand, swayed in his wooden saddle. He muttered words no one could understand.

The Arapaho rode out the way they had come in. A dog's head smouldered on the fire behind the trading post, and Louis Simmons still had not moved. Mary Lee looked back, once, and saw the dark forms of Caleb McGonigle and Angus MacPherson lying in the snow. She shuddered and prayed that her own death would be as quick.

"I wonder why Mama ran away," said Sally, more to herself than to her sisters.

Mary didn't say it aloud, but she was glad her mother did not stay there to see what the Indians did to them. She would rather be dead than have her mother see such terrible things.

"No talk," said Red Hawk and the Simmons girls said no more. They rode along, stunned with the memories of what had happened to them, prisoners not only of the Arapaho, but of their own sullied flesh, spoiled forever.

Mary Lee looked at Red Hawk's back, concentrated on the way he looked now, with his buffalo coat on, his fox cap pulled down over his ears. He had been the first to go between her legs, push into her, and after the others had finished, he had done it to her again.

She hated them, hated them all, but she hated that one, the leader, most of all.

But, even as she hated, she felt the power of the man who rode ahead of her. It was a power she did not understand and it frightened and confused her.

She thought of him and how it was when he was covering her, and she tried to drive the thought away, but it wouldn't go away and she wanted to scream, wanted to make them kill her so she wouldn't have to think about these things anymore.

Charity Newcastle saw Elizabeth Simmons stumble and fall. Charity was knocking snow off the woodpile, trying to find a few sticks for her firebox so she wouldn't have to cut more kindling.

"Lands, what is that woman up to?" she said aloud.

Luke Newcastle's wife was a thick-necked woman whose middle had so gone to girth that she appeared to have no waistline. She was beefy in the buttocks as well, but Luke never complained. He said she had a "classic" figure, and when she questioned him about it, he said "like them Greek and Roman women." She let it go at that, eating just what he ate, although she had heard terrible stories about potatoes from her Irish parents.

She was the closest to Elizabeth Simmons, probably because Charity was a listener. Elizabeth complained a lot, mostly about growing old and her hair turning gray and how Louis never seemed to pay any attention to her. Charity wondered why Elizabeth was in such a hurry that she fell so hard in the cold snow. She threw down the wood and hiked her skirts, floundered through crusty drifts to help her friend.

Elizabeth was out of breath and could only gasp as Charity struggled to get the woman on her feet.

"Land, Elizabeth, what has come over you? You've run yourself to foundering and not a breath in your lungs to tell me why."

Elizabeth, her face half-covered with snow, teetered on her feet while Charity brushed her off, held her up.

"Well, you just come in and set yourself at table, and I'll

heat us some fine tea and we'll talk about it when you catch your breath."

"Y—yes," Elizabeth stammered, but Charity did not like the wild look in her friend's eyes and told her not to talk, and not to worry.

The two women walked slowly to the Newcastle cabin. Elizabeth's lips were bluish from lack of oxygen and her face red from the cold and snow. When Charity felt her hands they were cold, and she rubbed them between her own as she helped the woman to the kitchen table.

"I'll be right back," said Charity. "I'll need some small wood for the firebox and we'll have that tea in no time. You just set and catch your breath, poor dear, I'll not be long."

The firebox glowed with coals and the wood caught fast. Charity said nothing as she scurried around the humble kitchen, poured melted snow water into the kettle and set it on the firebox. She spooned tea leaves into a small pot and set out cups. Elizabeth stared at nothing and did not notice any of this. Her breathing was labored and her throat rasped with the air she sucked in and let out in long, agonizing sighs. But, the color returned to her lips. The cabin was tight and the chinking snug and the pots all gleamed brightly from her polishing. Charity was proud of her kitchen and kept it spick and span, everything neatly hung on hooks or stacked on the counters, stored away methodically in the cupboards.

She poured the steaming water into the teapot and let the leaves steep as she sat down across from Elizabeth, finally, dreading what the woman had to say.

"There, now. I'll pour us some tea in a nonce and we'll find out what has you in such a state. Elizabeth?"

"Oh, Charity," said her friend and then her lips puckered up and she fought back the tears.

Charity reached across the table, touched Elizabeth's hand.

"Well, if it's weeping you want, maybe I'll weep with you, but for lands' sakes, Elizabeth, you must tell me what's troubling you? Is it Louis? One of the girls?"

Elizabeth seemed to be struggling with some demon inside herself. Her eyes rolled in their sockets and her lips quivered as if trying to form words. She made odd sounds in her throat, disturbing sounds that made Charity uneasy. Elizabeth's hand was as cold as a slab of iced venison and clammy with perspiration. The paleness of her skin was alarming as well, and Charity wondered if her friend was about to be taken with the fever, or worse, come down with a fit of some kind.

"Oh, God, I don't know," wailed Elizabeth, the words coming out all in one breath as if they had been pent up inside, fully formed, trapped in her larynx all this time. "My girls, Lou. . .the. . .Indians. . ."

Charity felt the floor sink from under her. Giddy, she blinked her eyes, tried to keep from showing signs of panic.

"Indians, Elizabeth? What Indians? Where?"

"Th—they come, they come. . .into the house. I ran. I—I didn't know what to do. They've killed them. They've done killed Lou and. . .oh my God, what have I done to deserve. . ."

Charity slumped to the back of her chair, held onto the table's edge to steady herself. It seemed as if the room was spinning around, rocking, teetering on a fulcrum. She felt suddenly lightheaded as the blood drained from her face. She thought she might faint, but the terror in her heart was too strong. She thought instantly that the Indians must have ridden down from the pass and slain everyone, the girls, Lou, perhaps Caleb, as well. She looked at Elizabeth in a new light. If what she said was true. . .

"Elizabeth. . ." she started, but saw that her words were unheard. Elizabeth stared beyond Charity, beyond the window, and her eyes shone with a haunting light, remained fixed in their sockets as though she was witnessing a scene of horror that was seared forever in her mind.

"No," Charity said quickly, "we—we musn't think that, dear woman. Oh no, perhaps the Indians just wanted a bit of food or a taste of Caleb's whiskey. We'll go," she sucked in a quick short breath for courage, "b–back there and see that everything's all right, that your man and children are all in their places. Perhaps they are looking for you now. Perhaps. . ." Her voice trailed away, faded as she saw Elizabeth slowly shake her head and continue to stare beyond anything in the kitchen, beyond anything on earth.

"I—I saw little Angus. I—I couldn't look at his face, but I saw him out in the cold. My—my voice just wouldn't speak. I wanted to tell him to run, but. . ."

"What? What's this about little Angus?" Charity felt the room go chill and she shivered. She knew she had been babbling to quell her own fears, had no intention of going to Elizabeth's to see, well, who knew what terrible things they might see? Maybe the Indians were real and still there, just waiting for them, waiting to take their scalps, or worse, defile them as she'd heard they did to white women. Babbling, yes, to hear the sound of her own voice, to know if the fear showed in it. She dreaded to hear any more, but an image of Angus floated up in her mind's boiling sea, and the chill drove deep inside her and she wished for a shawl to wrap around her head and shoulders, something of heavy wool and dark enough to shut out the light that filled the kitchen until it was stark and bright as a sick room.

A sound floated through the silence, ghostly as a graveyard wind. The two woman wondered what it meant at first, and their glances locked and froze. Then, they heard the sound again and Elizabeth sobbed, struggled to rise from her chair. Charity stood up, cupping a hand to her ear. The quiet was so strong, she was sure her hearing could not be trusted. Maybe, she thought, the sound was an Indian war cry. Perhaps the savages were coming to murder them, too, hunting them down like rabbits denned up in the rock crevices.

"It's the hunting horn," said Elizabeth, her voice soft and solemn. "The men have come back. Hear it?"

Charity laughed harshly, on the verge of hysteria. "Yes, yes, I heard it, Elizabeth. That would be Faron MacGregor's horn and I've never heard a sweeter sound on God's green earth."

"We must warn them," said Elizabeth.

"Warn them?"

"About the Indians."

"Yes, yes, of course, Elizabeth. I had forgotten."

Elizabeth stood, steady on her feet, and gave Charity a sharp-eyed glance of disapproval. "You don't believe me, do you, Charity Newcastle? You think I've made this all up."

"No, surely you mustn't think that of me, Elizabeth dear. It's just that, well, it all happened so fast, your coming here nigh out of your wits and telling me about the Indians, that I haven't had time for my senses to catch up with my hearing. Come, let us go out and meet the men. We'll tell them what you told me, and they'll get those savages before they run off. I'm sure the men will see to it that your kin come to no harm. Come, now, let us not waste another precious moment."

Charity spoke quickly to hide her doubts from herself and from Elizabeth. She avoided looking Elizabeth directly in the eyes. She took the woman's arm, careful not to knock over the teacups, and led her out the back door. The men were coming in from the south and there was plenty of time to warn them that savage Indians were about. The men, her man Luke, too, would make those savages sorry they ever came to the settlement, even if they meant no harm. Why, this was their land and the Utes had no business being on it, for whatever reason.

She guided Elizabeth to the clearing behind the cabin, then to the wide trail that passed beyond their stable shed and small barn, sliced through the valley along the creek. Her heart pounded from the exertion and the frosty air burned her lungs, but she was happy that the men had come back so soon.

The horn sounded again, closer this time.

Charity looked down the trail, trying to peer beyond the pine and spruce that bordered a portion of it, and saw that the sky was dark and leaden to the south. No wonder the men had come back so soon. Another storm was coming in, for certain, and the mountains were no place to be without warmth and shelter.

The creek gurgled as it rushed over the rocks, the water black against the snow clinging like ermine to its banks. "Here we are!" shouted Charity, stopping for breath. She shivered in the cold, heard the faint echoes of her voice die in the distance, smothered by the trees that stippled the slopes of the mountains that rose majestic above the valley.

CHAPTER 4

WILLIAM MacPHERSON picked up the stiffened corpse of his son, Angus. The grimy tracks of tears streaked his face, left smudges in the creases. Red-eyed, he looked around him at the others, looked at them helplessly, as if hoping they could explain why his son, his only son, was dead.

Young Gary Winder broke under the strain. He leaned against his father, Chollie, and sobbed violently. Chollie's face, reddened from the wind, hardened, his eyes seemed to sink deeper behind the puffy high cheekbones, eyes that crackled blue lightning. He put an arm around his son, dabbed at him with a snow-flocked mitten.

"Christ," murmured Luke Newcastle. Moments before, he had looked at what was left of Caleb McGonigle and had fought down the bile rising in his throat. Louis Simmons was alive, but stupefied. Jacques Berthoud and Jule Moreaux were pouring hot whiskey down his throat inside the trading post. Berle Campbell and Faron MacGregor stood in the small circle around Bill MacPherson, looking like snowy bears in their buffalo coats, their faces struck into masks of anger as if hammered in bronze.

"Take him home, Bill," said Faron, his voice booming even though it was down to a hoarse whisper. "We'll give him a proper burial in the morning."

"Be dark soon," said Luke, his voice cracking with emotion. "The missus and I'll come by, help Heather with the dressing of the boy."

"God damn them," Bill rasped. He lumbered off, carrying the body of little Angus, and the men watched him go, looked at his slumping shoulders and felt the same weight bear down on them.

The dark cloud that had followed the men from the south now loomed at the entrance to the valley. A few flakes of snow skittered on the swirling currents of air. Faron hunched deeper into his coat, pulled his beaver cap down tighter on his head. MacGregor was a lean, wiry man, who stood five feet nine in his stockings. He had hair the color of pale strawberry wine springing like thick wire from his scalp. The same colored hair sprouted from his nostrils, but otherwise, he was clean-shaven. He was older than the other men, nearly forty, and he liked to tell everyone how he had survived the brigades that trapped fur on the upper Missouri. "I played the pipes ever' day and scraped my whiskers off ever' morn." His voice still had a soft burr to it, the influence of his father who had been born in Aberdeen, Scotland, settled in Kentucky. "If ye want to keep the hair on your head," he had often said, "keep it off yer face." Most of the men followed his advice, but they chided him about the ragged mop that flowed from underneath his cap like rust-dyed twine.

"We'll have to put poor old Caleb somewhere the night," he said to the others. "Stiff as he is and the snow fallin', we'll never move him come light o' morn."

"Aye," said Berle Campbell, a ruggedly built Scot five years Faron's junior. "Chollie, you and Luke bear a hand and we'll take him to the storage room."

"Gary, you run along to home now," said Chollie quietly. "See to your mother and rub down the horses, give them some feed."

Gary nodded and walked down the packed trail, banished from the company of men. He was fourteen, tow-headed, blue-eyed, with eyebrows that were the color of cornsilk.

"The lad is taking it hard," said Berle.

"Aye, so do we all," muttered Faron under his breath. He looked at the body of Caleb McGonigle as the men lifted his corpse from the ground. He swiped at an unbidden tear and lumbered off toward the trading post to hold the door open for the men.

They buried little Angus beneath a cairn of stones the next morning. Caleb McGonigal was laid to rest in a small cave above the valley, the entrance sealed with a boulder pried from frozen ground. It was still snowing, had snowed all night, and the men knew they would have a hard time tracking the Arapaho. Louis Simmons stayed behind, conscious, but addled from the experience.

"I know what they did to my daughters," he said, "and if I were fit I'd go with you, kill every last one of those Indian skunks."

He stared at them stark-eyed as they rode off, shook his fist in the air.

"Cut their stones off!" he shouted, then broke down, weeping like a child. The men rode past him, unable to look at him without showing pity. The snow swirled around him for a long time after they disappeared from sight over the snow-packed pass where the Arapaho had ridden in an eternity ago.

Elizabeth finally came out of the cabin, where she had been scrubbing like a madwoman, and took her husband inside, out of the cold. She guided him to the big chair that he had built out of oak and tanned deerskin and sat him down. He buried his face in his hands and kept crying as his terrible thoughts worked at his brain like a worm, like a cancer, until she had to turn away and straighten a faded hunting print that hung crooked on the log wall. Elizabeth had done her weeping and now she prayed to herself as she had never prayed before. "Kill them, kill them," she murmured. "Kill them and bring my daughters back alive."

Jacques Berthoud broke trail. He was a hardy, usually cheerful Frenchman, who had trapped with Choteau's

American Fur when he was not much older than Gary Winder. When he left the last rendezvous he was only twenty, but looked thirty. Swarthy skinned, dark-haired, short of stature, he was hard as seasoned leather, impervious to cold or bad weather. He could track with the best of them, but he wondered how long before the blown places where the pony tracks were small dents in the snow would vanish.

Behind him, in single file, rode Bill MacPherson, Gary, and Chollie Winder who led three horses on a pack string that would be used as mounts for the Simmons girls, Faron MacGregor, Luke Newcastle, and Berle Campbell. Jules Moreaux brought up the rear, his worn .54 caliber Hawken in its fringed buckskin sleeve lying across the pommel of his saddle.

Jules was half-Sioux, his mother being an Unkpapa woman called Pretty Beads. Jules had run away from the Sioux after his father was killed for taking another man's wife, and he had never returned. A missionary couple had taught him to read and write, corrected his bad English until he was able to speak without much of an accent. He forgot most of the Sioux language, learned a little Spanish in Taos. He had married a young Santa Fe woman in 1845, who had turned out to be barren. He was a bitter, silent man, befitting his image of himself as an outcast from both the white and Indian worlds. Jacques had taken Jules and his wife, Maria, away from Santa Fe to save Jules from a short life of drunken fighting in the *cantinas*. Jules had become the best hunter of the bunch and the odd assortment in Sky Valley made him feel comfortable. Jules was taciturn most of the time, but when he drank whiskey, he loosened up, told wild tales of living with the Unkpapa as a boy. The Scotsmen didn't hold that against him. "A mon is bairn whar' he be bairn and he dinna choose his parentage," Faron MacGregor once expressed, speaking for all of the Scots in the settlement. "Jules is his own mon and he's good to his bonnie wife. I'll gladly make him welcome at my fire for all o' that."

Beyond the pass, Jacques lost the trail. The snowstorm worsened, and the men milled around, rode in circles. The storm turned into a blizzard until even the tracks of the men riding in circles became obliterated. Berthoud sought shelter, but they were on the flat, and rode half-blind. Finally, he dismounted where the spruce trees became thick and began cutting boughs that he stacked high to shut off the wind. The others followed suit, and when they had a shelter under a clump of spruce that grew close together, Jacques and Chollie gathered the makings for a fire from deadwood dug out of the snow.

"I'll get the coal oil, Pa," said Gary. They always brought oil to start a quick fire if the weather got bad. If a man fell into a creek in this weather he might have to set a tree on fire quick, or freeze to death.

Chollie nodded, noting that the boy had tethered the extra horses in a good place.

The fire, fueled by the coal oil, blazed high.

"There is no chance to find zem," said Berthoud. "Zey have gone to ze ground, into a beeg hole."

"I ken ye're right," said Faron MacGregor. "We'd best warm ourselves, then go back through the pass 'fore night catches us."

Gary Winder shivered in the cold, hunkered near the fire, trying to warm pink wet fingers. He nodded, and his teeth chattered, clacking like a box full of dominoes. His father, Chollie, pulled a smoking boot away from the fire. Luke Newcastle trudged in with his arms full of squaw-wood ripped from the pine trees. He threw the dried branches on the fire and they caught, blazed brightly, threw out heat that melted the falling snow for a few seconds.

"What if we do turn back?" asked Bill MacPherson. "Say we wait out the storm, then what? Any chance we can still track those Injuns?" He looked at Jacques Berthoud through the wall of flames. Jacques shrugged, twisted his head to look up into the teeth of the storm.

"We don' ever find dose Injun," he said. "Dey gone now. Maybe we wait for spring, eh?"

"Spring? Hell, they'll be a thousand miles from here by then," Bill said bitterly.

"Maybe not," said Berle. "They got to hole up too, same as us. I say we go on down to home, wait out the storm, then pack out, see if we can pick up their trail."

Jacques shook his head again.

"Dese Injun, *non*. Dey plenty bad. Dey go away like smoke. With ze white women, dey find big camp, hide out like timber wolf."

"You sayin' they'll stay to the high country?" Berle asked.

"Eh, mebbe," replied Berthoud.

The men argued back and forth for a few moments. Finally, Luke broke in. "What about Horne?" he said.

"What?" exclaimed MacGregor. "What are ye sayin', mon?"

"You're all saying those Arapaho can't be tracked, but I bet that damned Horne could find 'em for us."

"Horne's not at his diggings," said MacPherson. "I didn't see no smoke back there in the trees. He took his stock down to the flat for winter pasture. No good reason for him to come back. Less'n he's going to trap another winter."

"He'll be back. He don't like bein' down on the flat. This storm will bring him in like it did us," said Luke.

No one spoke for several moments. The men looked at the fire, at the falling snow, everyplace but at one another. No one liked to talk about Horne. He kept to himself, they seldom saw him, stayed out of his way when they did.

"Jackson Horne," mused Campbell. "I wonder what he would say about all that happened, about us coming up here like this?"

"I don't give a damn what he'd say," said MacPherson. "If he's the man to track these murdering bastards, then I say let's talk to him."

"Horne wouldn't give us the time of day," said Chollie Winder. "But I bet he knows Injuns better'n anybody here 'ceptin' Moreaux."

Jules said nothing. Everyone looked at him, though, as if seeing him for the first time. Suddenly he felt alien again, an outcast, an outsider. He turned his back to them, warmed his bottom by the fire.

"Well, Jules, what do you say?" asked Luke, pointedly. "You think Jackson Horne could track these Injuns? Could you track them?"

Jules turned around slowly, took a deep breath. Snow blew over the dwindling fire, whipping the flames, sending a fountain of sparks flying into the air.

"You want to know what I think," he said slowly, "and I will tell you a thing. Horne. He is very wild, I think. Once, when I lived with the Sioux, we had a very bad winter, like this one. There was no fresh meat in camp. We could not hunt on the prairie. We had stayed too long above the place where the Yellowstone meets the Missouri and the people were cold and hungry. The head men talked in the big lodge and they said they must hunt or they would all die. The babies were already crying, yes, and the women were growing thin so that their husbands could eat and stay strong to hunt.

"We went out hunting the elk and the deer. We all hunted in different directions, two, three men together. I hunted with a man called Thumping Bull, who was married to Sleeping Water, my mother's sister. There was much snow, like this, and the tracking was hard. We saw an elk track, but did not follow it. I did not say anything because Thumping Bull was my uncle and I respected him. He came upon the tracks of a wolf and he ran after them. I had to run hard to keep up with him. The tracks were fresh and not much snow in them. My uncle stopped running, walked slow when the tracks got fresher. I asked him why we had not tracked the elk, but were only tracking this one little wolf. He said that the elk were lost to his eyes, that he could not see them. He said he could not smell them. 'The wolf knows where the elk has gone,' he said. 'Let the wolf be our eyes and ears and nose.'

"We found the wolf very soon. He had a calf down, was tearing out its stomach. We found many elk in a good place and we shot three of them with arrows. We put blood and fresh meat in our bellies and cut up the meat. When we found the others and took them back, they helped us carry the meat back to camp."

"What are you saying, Jules?" asked Chollie.

"This Horne. He is the wolf. He maybe could find the Arapaho. I don't think he will hunt them, though."

"Why?" asked Luke.

Moreau shrugged, turned his back to the fire again. "Because he has no reason to look for them," he said softly. But every man there knew that Jules was just saying that so he could pull away from the talk. There was a common fear among them of this man Horne, but no one could put a name to it. If Jules knew something more about the man he was not saying anything and maybe the others were glad about that, because, down deep, they did not want to know those things he kept to himself.

"We'll pay him," said Bill MacPherson. The moment he said it, he knew he was just grabbing at straws in a whirlpool.

The men fell silent again, and Faron MacGregor walked away from the fire, caught up his horse. "We'll bide no more here," he said.

The other men followed him, picked up frozen reins and climbed into slick wet saddles. Chollie tightened his cinch, gathered the riderless horses, checked their pack strings. The men rode out of the trees and back onto the snowy trail. They had the wind at their backs now, and slumped over in their saddles, they looked like beaten men going back to a prison from whence they had recently escaped. The snow blew out their tracks until there was little trace of them ever having been on the trail of the Arapaho.

When they reached the valley, they trudged into Caleb's trading post and lit the lanterns, built a fire in the potbellied stove.

"We'll talk to Horne when he gets back," said Bill MacPherson and the men nodded in agreement. Luke slapped him on the back and turned away when he saw the tears spring up in Bill's eyes.

"We'll get them," said Berle. "We'll bring the girls back, too."

His words sounded hollow in the silence of the room. Caleb's goods lay on shelves, all neatly stacked again as if his ghost had returned to tidy up one last time.

CHAPTER 5

JACKSON HORNE heard the fluting call of the young bull, hunkered deeper into the brush. He grunted into a buffalo horn, made a sound like a cow elk, *mwuuuuuum, mwuuuuuohm.* The sounds came out soft and pleading. He heard the brush crash as the young bull came nearer. Horne let the buff horn slide down to his side, pushed it around to his back where it hung on leather thongs, out of the way.

He brought the .54 caliber Hawken with its percussion lock, up to his shoulder. He pulled the trigger slightly, cocked back the hammer until the sear engaged. He waited, listening to the crackle of brush, the hooves sliding on snow as the elk approached. The animal loped into the small clearing, its head high, antlers majestically laid back as it sniffed the air. The elk stopped, pawed the snow, and looked around for the cow and the lone bull whose bugle had brought him to this place.

The elk turned, tossed its rack impatiently. Horne took the shot. He held the rifle tight against his shoulder, drew a short breath, held it. His finger squeezed the trigger once he steadied the buckhorn sight on the animal's vital area, just behind the left shoulder, less than midway up its flank. The Hawken bucked, kicked against him as a hundred grains of black powder exploded. Horne's view of the elk was blocked by the cloud of white powder that billowed out from the muzzle of his rifle. For several moments he could not see, as the moisture in the air held the smoke down. Gradually, the wind blew the smoke into wisps and he saw the elk, several yards from where he had hit it. Blood crimsoned the fresh snow where it had run. Horne reached for the buffalo horn and called softly to it. The animal fell onto its folded forelegs, held steady. Horne reloaded quickly, poured fine-grained black powder into a brass tube he used for a measure. He tapped the stock to settle the powder, took a .530 ball and a greased patch of cloth measuring about fifteen thousands of an inch from his possibles pouch. He placed the patch on the muzzle, the ball atop it, and rammed it partially down the barrel with a short starter made from a brass-handled bunghole starter. He cut the patch off clean at the muzzle and took his ramrod from the rifle and seated the ball snug in the chamber. He did not cap the rifle from the leather capper that hung on another thong from his neck, but stood up, walked slowly toward the mortally wounded bull.

Horne looked at the blood trail carefully. There were a lot of crimson splotches on the snow, more splatters on the gaunt, skeletal underbrush, and some of it was pink, frothy.

"Caught a lung," he said to himself. But he knew he had struck the heart, too, and possibly taken out a chunk of liver. He stood near the animal, watched as it struggled to rise to its feet. The bull's mane was streaked with ejaculate and he stank of the rut. Piss stained his hind legs and there were suspicious swirls along his belly, stiffened spots of sperm residue.

The elk fell on its side. The blood spurting from its side stopped as its eyes glazed over in a fixed, blind glare.

Horne set his Hawken against a tree and drew his knife. He made the cuts—belly, neck, groin, took out the anus, the entrails, gutted the animal expertly. His breath made fog as he labored at his task, took his time, never hurrying as he removed the windpipe, cut off the head. It would have been easier stringing the animal up with rope, using a block and tackle, but there was no time. The storm upon him was serious and he faced a hard ride back to the valley, straight into the knifing north wind.

He skinned the elk's carcass, laid out the green hide and

began quartering. He took the body off at the neck, all four legs off above the knee joint. He laid the meat in the center of the hide, then bundled it all up, ran sinew through holes he cut with his knife, tied all the strands tight. It took him twenty minutes to bring up his horse and the pack mules. Two of these were already staggering under the weight of fresh elk, and there was a mule deer carcass slung over one of the panniers, lashed down with rope tied in a double diamond hitch.

"Gideon, you sonofabitch, easy," growled Horne as the big brown mule balked at the end of his pack string. Horne separated the mule from the others—a small wiry black jenny he called Delilah, and a brown jack named Samson. He led Gideon over to a pine near the quartered elk and snubbed the mule up close. He tightened the cinches on the pannier, then walked to his horse, a sorrel gelding he called Tony. He dug rope and a strap out of his saddlebags and untied a small square of buffalo hide from behind his cantle. He rigged the elk, hefted the bundle close to Gideon. He slung the attached ropes over the animal's back and slipped to the opposite side. He worked the bundle up to the wooden pannier, then used the sinew loops to secure it to the posts. He secured the other side in the same way, then rigged his diamond hitch, putting the small patch of buff hide under Gideon's belly so the ropes wouldn't worry him.

Horne's smoky breath came out thick by the time he was finished and had tied the mule back on the pack string. He grained the animals with the last few handfuls he had, then mounted Tony and set off toward Sky Valley. He looked back through the swirling snow, felt satisfied. He had meat for the winter and his belly was full from a breakfast of fresh meat, the heart and haunch of a timberwolf killed at dawn as it tried to tear the mule deer carcass from Samson's back.

Horne hung the Hawken from his saddlehorn by a thong attached to the waist of the stock. It was within easy reach and his capper was tucked inside his sheepskin jacket, warm against his chest.

The rider was a big man by any standards, topping six foot and some three inches, with wide, brawny shoulders, and a slim waist that gutted out in winters, after the hunt, but trimmed down in summer and fall when he rode the high country, lived off the land like the Indian. Horne had come to the valley long before the others, but he did not consider it his own. He didn't figure a man had much right to land that was free. He kept to himself, raising and breaking good horses, trapping for meat and skins in the winter months, more out of habit than necessity, but traded at McGonigle's when he had to. He never said much, and his deep blue eyes didn't show much, either. He kept his face scraped, except during the long winter months when he didn't bother and let a beard cover his square jaw, frame his chiseled high cheekbones.

For some reason, Horne had an uneasy feeling about going back to the valley. He had cut sign two days before, and from the tracks he knew that the Scots were hunting, the Frenchies, too. But, they hadn't made any meat, he knew that, and he knew they must have had to go back before the storm hit. The elk and deer were already moving to the lowlands. The young bull had been luck. He had taken the big ones much lower down, and the muley deer had just gotten off its bed at the wrong time, taken a drink out of the Poudre when Horne was upwind. There would be little game, if any, the rest of the season, and such poor stock that couldn't get out would die in this, or the next, winter storm.

The first snows had come early, before the elk rutted, and now, with this second storm on them, the bulls had stopped rutting until they could get to lower ground. All except for that young bull, Horne surmised, who had gotten its signals all mixed up.

Horne rode into the valley some five hours later, his butt

sore, his knees locked from his feet being in the stirrups for so long a stretch. The horse and mules were weary, and so was he. He broke off the main trail, headed for his cabin at the far edge of the valley. He could not see the smoke rising from cabin chimneys, but he smelled the acrid sting of burning wood in his nostrils. The snow fell hard now, driven by the north wind and he saw, in places where the snow had not drifted, that the men had returned. There were faint impressions, hollow indentations made by hoofprints that were fading fast in the steady buildup of flakes.

Someone hailed him when he rode within fifty yards of the Winder cabin. Horne reined up, tried to peer through the swirling snow. It was late afternoon and the blotted-out sun did not give much light. He saw the glow of lamplight in the Winder cabin windows, and a dark figure running toward him.

"Mister Horne! Mister Horne! Wait!"

The boy scrambled through the drifts, splashing up snow from underheel in flying chunks. He waved his arms frantically as if afraid Horne would ride on. Horne waited, his lips curled in a faint sign of annoyance.

"Is—is that you, Mister Horne?" the boy panted, out of breath. He stood there in the fading light of afternoon, shielding his eyes from the falling snow.

Horne saw that it was the Winders boy. He couldn't recall his name.

"What do you want, boy?"

"You gotta come quick, up to Cale. . .up to the trading post. There's been trouble. Everybody's up there and they want to talk to you real bad."

"Trouble?"

"Injuns. Mister McGonigle and little Angus. The Simmons girls. Mister Simmons ain't hurt bad, though. It was just real bad. You gotta come. They told me to keep an eye out for you."

Although the boy didn't make much sense, Horne knew

that something undoubtedly had happened. He thought about it. It was over another two hour's ride to his cabin and small spread, less than that to the trading post. The meat would keep, but he had wanted to hang the carcasses before nightfall. Well, he reasoned, maybe there would yet be time.

"I'll go there, boy; ah, George, isn't it?"

"Gary, Mister Horne. I'm Gary Winder, Chollie's boy."

"You run on ahead, tell 'em I'm comin' and to make it quick. I got meat to put up."

"Yes, sir. Thank you, sir." Relieved, Gary ran off, cutting through the trees, disappearing into the swirling mass of blowing snowflakes. Horne turned his horse, followed the slight depression that marked the road to McGonigle's. He wondered what had happened there. He tried to place the Simmons girls in his mind, but he couldn't remember them much. Little Angus, though, he could remember. The boy had come down to his cabin a time or two, peered at him from behind trees, had watched him at chores. Small, thin boy, looked like he was half-starved. Big eyes. Indians? What in hell would Indians be doing in the valley this time of year? Horne shook his head, shrugged deeper into his sheepskin coat as a sudden blast of wind chilled him to the bone.

The windows in the Simmons cabin and at McGonigle's trading post glowed copper, flickered with lantern light when Horne rode up. He saw a silhouette at the front window of the store as he dismounted. He tied Tony and the pack mules to the hitchrail out front, climbed the four steps to the porch. He stomped the snow off his boots and slapped his hat against his thigh before opening the door.

The big room was warm. The men of the valley stood against the counters or sat around the potbellied stove. They stared at Horne as he strode across the room, came to a halt a few feet from them. The snow clinging to his clothes began to melt. Water streamed from his boots, sought the grooves and cracks in the floor. The aroma of hot cider permeated the room, mingled with the other scents of dry goods, leather, beans, coffee, dried vegetables, burning wood and candlewax. Lanterns cast shadows, radiated orange light that limned the gaunt faces of the waiting men.

"Evenin'," said Luke Newcastle. Horne looked at him and Luke cleared his throat. Horne didn't like Newcastle, and didn't try to hide his feelings for the man. Sometimes he got a feeling for a man, and he had disliked Newcastle the moment he had set eyes on him.

"You have a good hunt?" asked Chollie Winder. Horne swung his gaze to Chollie, saw his boy again, standing in his father's shadow, gape-mouthed, eyes bright as a coon's. He looked at the others then, saw Bill MacPherson, Jacques Berthoud, Jules Moreaux, Berle Cambell, Faron MacGregor, Louis Simmons, who sat on a pile of trade blankets, his head swathed in a bandage.

"Fair," said Horne. "The boy tells me you had trouble here."

Luke cleared his throat again. Bill MacPherson winced, blinked his eyes. The other men looked at the floor, shifted their feet, swallowed, as Horne raked them with a questioning glance.

"Damn right we had trouble," said Simmons. "I held them off long as I could, but they kilt Caleb and little Angus and took my daughters. Tried to kill this old soul, but the good lord didn't see fit to take me. I tell you, Horne, I'da kilt 'em all if I coulda gotten to my rifle."

Horne knew the man was babbling. The others looked at him with pitying glances and Simmons was looking at no one. His voice was hoarse, weak, and the man's eyes shone with an inner madness that was plain to see. Luke Newcastle pulled away from the counter, came up behind Simmons, put a hand on his shoulder.

"Horne, we tried to track 'em," he said. "The storm blew us back. What Lou says is so. Those skunks took Lou's daughters, all three of 'em, and we buried a boy and a man. We're just wonderin' if you could help us."

The way he said it, Horne knew the man spoke for all of them. He saw the desperation in their faces. Lou Simmons was scared, backtracking some to prove he wasn't a coward, but Horne figured he had been scared out of his wits when the Indians rode in.

"How many, what kind?" asked Horne.

"They was seven of 'em," said Lou. "Caleb said they was Arapaho."

Horne's eyebrows twitched, bristled like caterpillars.

"Anybody else see them?"

"The missus," replied Simmons. "Oh, they was Arapaho all right, painted for war. They ate Caleb's dogs, too."

Horne took a deep breath, sucking the air in through his nostrils. A trickle of melted snow streamed down the back of his neck, icy cold. He took off his gloves, wiped his neck.

"Will you help us, Horne?" asked Chollie.

"Depends. What do you want to do?"

"Kill them," squawled Simmons. "Get my daughters back safe and sound."

The others nodded.

"How?" said Horne.

"We were hoping you could tell us," said Luke. All of the men chorused yesses and nodded their heads. Horne saw that Jules Moreaux was watching them with hawk eyes, hooded, unblinking.

Chollie nudged his son and whispered into the boy's ear. Gary rolled an empty keg out from behind the counter, lifted it. He carried it to Horne, set it down next to him.

"Set down, Mister Horne," said Chollie. "Listen to us, at least. We don't know much about the Arapaho and we can't just let this go by. Even if you just tell us what to do. . ."

Horne considered it. "Not much you can do about such," he said softly, unbuttoning his coat. He tucked his gloves in a side pocket, looked for a place to put it. Gary took it from him, hung it on the wall where it dripped, making a puddle on the floor. Horne sat down on the keg, closed his eyes, rubbed them. "Arapaho is their own people," he said slowly, "and not many tribes take to them. They been driven out of every place they ever been and they hate Utes worse'n white people, love dog more than cowmeat."

"Goddamnit!" exclaimed MacPherson, "I don't want to hear about the goddamned Injuns. What in hell you goin' to do about my boy?"

"Steady, William," said MacGregor, "dinna fash yoursel'. Let the mon talk."

MacPherson glared at MacGregor, then at Horne. His jaw jutted out in sudden belligerence.

"Well, Horne, go ahead, then," said MacPherson tightly his tones laden with anger.

"Simmons," said Horne, "you tell me what those Arapaho looked like, what they did. Don't lag on it any, and don't put any frills on it."

Lou swelled up his chest, sat up straighter on the pile of blankets.

He spoke rapidly, detailing everything he saw. He spoke only to Horne, but the others listened raptly. He told where the Indians had ridden in from, and what they did. He described their warpaint and weapons in detail when Horne broke in to question him. He described their clothes and how they had killed the dogs and Caleb.

"I was a-tryin' for my rifle when they put out my lamp for a spell," he finished. "I didn't see 'em kill little Angus. . . ."

"Those Arapaho were way out of their country," said Horne. "Likely they were hunting Utes. Maybe got drove out, come down here lookin' for food. Bad medicine for them to get into the whiskey. Probably why they went after the women. Well, they're holed up somewheres, just like us. They could be tracked when the storm breaks."

Horne rose from the nail keg, strode to the wall. He took his coat off the hook, slipped it on.

"You gonna help us, Horne?" MacPherson asked pointedly.

Horne stepped toward them, walked in close to the assemblage around the stove. He squared his hat, pulled his gloves from his pocket.

"Arapaho call themselves *Inuna-ina*," he said. "'Our people.' Loners mostly, but sometimes they take up with the Cheyenne. Once learned some bad habits from the Blackfoot. The Sioux call 'em 'blue cloud men,' for some reason. They hate Utes like poison, and don't have much use for white men. I figger they lost some men fighting, maybe some ponies, too. They'll want to go back and lick their wounds and the white women will keep 'em peaceful for a time,"

Simmons' face flushed a ruddy crimson. The others looked at him in embarrassment.

"That's a hell of a thing to say," said Newcastle. "Just what's your point, Horne?"

"That one Arapaho, the one Simmons said was the leader. Sounds like someone I knew once. Young buck name of Red Hawk. Always was one to go against the grain. He'll fight and if you press him too hard he might kill those girls. If he does, and you chase him off, he'll be back. And he won't bring a half-dozen braves with him next time, either."

"That mean you ain't agonna help us?" asked Luke.

"I just did," said Horne, and turned on his heel as the men stared at him with mouths open. He stalked toward the door.

"Where you goin', Horne?" asked Simmons, a puzzled tone in his voice.

Horne paused, turned around. "I got meat to put up."

"Would you want to be sellin' any o' that?" asked Faron, on a note of practicality. "We're more'n willin' to pay."

"I don't need anything," said Horne. "But, you're welcome to what meat I have left after I stock my own larder." Once again, he turned to leave.

Lou Simmons' voice stopped him. Simmons stood up, teetered for a moment. His stare fixed on Horne's trail-grizzled face as he asked the hunter pointblank: "What did they call you, Mister Horne?"

"Who?"

"The Arapaho, that's who."

"They called me Gray Wolf," said Horne and stalked into the night without another word, leaving a silence behind him that was hard as stone.

"He's a bastard," said Newcastle bitterly, and his eyes burned with a hatred that bored through them from deep within him.

"*He's a man,*" said Jules Moreaux softly.

CHAPTER 6

THE storm broke during the night. Horne was up early, shoveling snow away from his door, cutting a path to the log stable, setting out feed for his horse and mules. It was bitterly cold, and icicles hung from the roofs of the house and outbuildings. Smoke drifted in a lazy spiral from his chimney. A jay squawked from a nearby fir, and a squirrel barked in a chittering, long-winded reply. Horne noticed all the fresh tracks and took pleasure in cataloging, in his mind, the animals that had made them.

Horne stuffed some cherry tobacco in his jaw and walked to the glade where he always kept his meat. After he made that last fateful rendezvous, at Horse Creek on the Green River, in '33, he had drifted south, living off the land. He had trapped some, traded his pelts in Taos, glad to be free of the politics that pervaded the fur trade. He was just twenty-three when he left Andy Drips at his camp on Horse Creek, run away like a coward from all the men he had known, trapped with for nigh a half-dozen years. He had come to this valley, below Cameron Pass, left it twice, then had come back to stay. Nearly ten years of hiding from himself now, and people crowding him once again. . .

He had stripped trees, nailed cross-braces, rigged blocks and tackle, kept them greased. His meat hung high off the ground, safe from bears, wolves, porcupines, rats and other critters. The lodgepole pines were barked and slick, sturdy enough for his purposes. The glade was laced with tracks, bear and wolf mostly, but the meat he had hung the night before was safe, curing nicely. Horne's stomach growled. He spat a brownish stream of tobacco at the base of the tree where the mule deer carcass hung, set down his Hawken, squatted to read the track of a small bear that had tried to climb up the tree during the night. Four hours old, by the looks of it. The sun was just beginning to crust its edges and there was blown snow in its hollow; just a trace.

That business of the night before bothered him. The men were desperate, looking for trouble. He could understand that. He had felt the same way a time or two. Revenge. It could cloud a man's mind until he couldn't see the danger. Best to stop and do some hard thinking before chasing after trouble. Red Hawk was trouble.

That last long trip with Andy Drips was a hell of a journey, not all bad, but bad enough. He had been with the other free trappers up on the Yellowstone, rode with them to Cache Valley. There, he had met Drips and Fontanelle. Another party from American Fur had wintered there, too. It had been cold as a hardrock miner's butt, but he joined up with Drips and Lucien Fontanelle, hunted on the Snake that next spring. A little after mid-June, he and about thirty men, twenty of them Flatheads, had gone to St. Louis. Drips asked him to go with them on the next expedition, but they were late getting off, because Fontanelle, in Bellevue, didn't get the supplies upriver until the first of October.

The horses were in bad shape, and there was poor forage, so they spent that winter near the Laramie River at the foot of the Black Hills. It was near the last of April when they got to Muddy Creek. The twenty-fourth, he recollected. The Muddy ran into the Bear River and they trapped some on their way to Pierre's Hole. Didn't get there until mid-June, too early for rendezvous. Andy did some trading with the Indians until they had the fight in July with the Gros Ventres. Horne laughed when he thought about that. It could have been worse. Andy took a ball through his hat and it clipped a lock of his hair clean through. Horne left Drips after he and Vanderburgh went across the Tetons to meet Fontanelle and Provost on the headwaters of the Green. He didn't find out until later that Drips and Vanderburgh took off after Fitzpatrick and Bridger, went into Blackfoot country where Vanderburgh was killed.

Horne met up with Andy in late October and wintered with him at the forks of the Snake River. They broke camp near the end of March, in '33, and had a good spring hunt. They trapped Lewis Fork, Gray's Hole, Salt River, Pierre's Hole and Jackson's Hole, got to Horse Creek the first week of June. Bonneville had built him a fort there and the boys from Rocky Mountain Fur had to camp down on the Green. Drips camped at the mouth of Horse Creek. Horne left him there, hadn't seen nor heard of him since. Too many trappers, not enough game. The never-ending politics. The death of a good friend, and the grief that had followed him all these years. And something else, something he could not put a name to, a horror of a thing that haunted him still. Horne had had enough of it.

He had run, run hard, and kept checking his backtrail to see if someone, someday, would come for him and call him to account. He had run way past those times, all right. But now he wondered if a man could outrun himself. For what he had thought he had left behind in those far mountains, had buried there forever, was still with him. He was carrying the horror of it still. And that other thing, with the Arapaho. Now that was back on him. Red Hawk. *I should have killed him,* Horne thought. *I should have killed him right off.*

He spat again, tucked the tobacco cud on the other side of his mouth. The sun crawled across the sky toward its noon position, and the trees began their slow drip as the snow flocking their branches began to melt. Horne picked up his rifle, rubbed the barrel. He was about to walk back to his cabin, when he heard them coming.

He knew what they were after. Trouble.

Chollie, Bill, Faron, Jacques and Luke rode through the thick timber, following the trail that Horne had made the night before. They had been chosen by a vote of the others to talk to Horne one last time, try to persuade him to accompany them in their search for Red Hawk's band of Arapaho.

"You think he'll come with us?" asked Chollie. He rode alongside Faron, at the rear of the small column. His frosty breath plumed out of his mouth in wisps of patchy fog. Tree shadows slashed across his face, the heavy wool-lined Mackinaw coat he wore. The coat was patched at the elbows, frayed at the collar. Like the others, he had a brace of pistols slung from his saddlehorn, a rifle in a cowhide scabbard dangling from thongs attached to cinch-rings. He carried a bedroll wrapped in a dull gray slicker tied back of the cantle.

"I have me dooubts," said MacGregor, elongating his "o's" in his thick Scot's brogue. "The mon's not one of us. He goes his own way."

"The sonofabitch," muttered MacPherson.

"Take it easy, Bill," said Luke. "We might oughtta wait and see what Horne says."

They had agreed that it would be better if Horne came along. He was a more experienced tracker, knew more about the Arapaho than any of them. They had argued long into the night until Elizabeth Simmons came and got Lou, took him home. She had called them a pack of cowards for not staying out on the trail during the blizzard and letting her daughters suffer. Her words had stung and the men had decided to leave as soon as the storm broke.

"I do not think you will make Horne do what he do not want to do," said Berthoud.

"That's for damn sure," said Luke, riding in the lead. "I think the man's hiding up here, runnin' from somethin' or somebody. I'll bet that more'n one starpacker's lookin' for that sonofabitch."

"Luke, you take care to what you say," said MacPherson.

"Well, I don't trust the bastard," Luke said.

"Jest see that ye hold yer tongue," warned Faron MacGregor.

None of the men had ever seen Horne's place up close.

They knew it by the smoke from its chimney, and some who had hunted the rimrock had seen glimpses of it, through the trees.

They rode up on the cabin in silence. Only the sounds of the horses' hooves breaking through snow and the creak of leather marred the quiet of late morning. They saw the smoke first, smelled it. Horne's horse nickered at them, but they couldn't see it. One of the mules brayed, sounding like a distant foghorn.

Horne stepped out of the trees before the men reached his cabin.

Luke hauled in on the reins of his dusky black gelding. The others rode up to surround him on both sides. They looked down at Horne, whose gloved hands covered the muzzle of his rifle as it stood on its buttplate on the top of his boot.

Horne's eyes flickered as his glance took in their trappings, their weapons.

"You come to see me," he said flatly. "Say what it is you got to say."

"You don't make it easy, Horne," said Luke.

"All we ask is that you listen to us, Horne," said Faron MacGregor. "Women's lives are at stake."

"I'll listen," said Horne. "Make it quick."

"Look, Horne," said Luke, trying to keep his voice calm. "The Simmons girls are young; the oldest twenty-two and Mary Lee almost eighteen. None of us likes to think what those Injuns might be doin' with 'em. Missus Simmons is just heartbroke and Lou, he's plumb crazy with worry. These are people, Horne. White people. Young, innocent girls. We want you to ride with us and track those scalpin', murderin', thievin', sonsofbitches, bring those little girls back to their folks before they're sullied or kilt."

Horne spat a stream of tobacco juice at the front hooves of Newcastle's horse. The snow steamed as a brown stain ate through it. "That it?" he asked.

"We know you can track the Arapaho. We know you know

more about 'em than we do," said Luke. "Damnit, man, we need you. Can't you give up a few days of your time to help us? Hell, you knew McGonigle. Maybe you saw little Angus. Those murderin' bastards killed them in cold blood."

"I reckon they killed 'em, all right," said Horne. "Can't do much about that."

"No, but you can help save three women, girls really, who don't deserve to be killed. . .or raped."

"Likely, they'll live," said Horne, "seein' as how Red Hawk took 'em with him. Imagine he did all the rapin' 'fore he took 'em."

"You sonofabitch!" exclaimed MacPherson. "They killed my boy! You act like you don't. . ."

MacGregor touched a hand to Bill's shoulder.

"Easy, mon," he whispered. "Dinna gi' yoursel' in a fret."

"Horne, what's your answer? We'll back you up all the way. You can leave as soon as you find them for us. We'll take care of the rest. You can be back here in two, three days." Luke laid it all out, breathed a sigh as he rocked backward in his saddle. "Will you come with us?"

"No," said Horne. "You may live up in the mountains, same as me, but you're all pilgrims, pure and plain."

"You wouldn't do anything to save the girls?" snapped MacPherson.

Horne picked up his rifle, rested it on his shoulder as if to leave.

"Didn't say that, MacPherson. I know you're grieved over the boy. I saw him some. McGonigle was a good enough man, I reckon. I seen a lot of folks come and go. That happens, you say goodbye and get on with your own livin'. You can't bring your boy back and you can't go layin' blame at other folks' doors."

"Wait a minute, Horne," said Bill. "Just what did you say?"

Horne spat the cud of tobacco out, wiped his mouth with his sleeve. He paused, looked at the men again, staring at each one in turn, inspecting them as if he was an army commander in the field. He shook his head.

"I can track the Arapaho, likely," he said. "If you got caught in the storm, so did they. They won't be far. They got a day, day and a half on you, maybe."

"So, will you come with us?" interjected Luke.

"No. I'll not ride with any of you," replied Horne.

"Why not?" snapped MacPherson.

"Look at yourselves. You're all spoiling for a fight. You got blood in your eyes, revenge in your craws. Red Hawk will have scouts out. The bunch of you will make so much noise, he can't miss you. Count on it. The Arapaho will slip up on you so quiet you'll never know how you died."

The men looked at one another. Newcastle wiped sweat beads off his forehead. Chollie licked his dry lips. Faron MacGregor cleared his throat. MacPherson blinked, lost some of the set from his jaw.

"You're sayin' what, Horne?" asked Luke. "One man's better than eight or nine?"

"Maybe. One man's harder to keep track of. You all get out there and the arguin' starts. One of you'll want to go one way, the rest another. One will want to fight, the others will want to wait. Half of you will want to go on, the other half will want to quit."

"The mon makes sense, Luke," said MacGregor. "Aye."

"Are you sayin' you'll go then?" asked Luke. "Alone?"

"I'll go. No promises. No guarantees." Horne wondered why they would pick a man like Newcastle to speak for them. The man had the backbone of a snake.

"We got to talk this over, Horne," rasped MacPherson.

"No," Horne replied. "You men pack that fresh meat back to your families. I'll get my possibles and make the ride. Take it or leave it."

Horne turned, started to walk toward his cabin.

"Hold on there, Horne," said MacPherson. "I got a question for you." The belligerence was still there, boiling in him. Horne saw it, and leaned his rifle against the patchy bark of a pine. MacPherson rode up, his face blotchy from emotion. It was plain his blood was running hot. He handled his horse rough, pulling the bit hard against its mouth when he reined up. He leaned over, the veins on his neck thick as a hemp rope.

"How do we know we can trust you?" Bill asked.

"What do you mean by that?"

"I mean there are three white girls with those Injuns and you don't have any woman in your cabin, Horne."

Horne reached out, grabbed MacPherson's collar with both hands and jerked him from his horse. Bill lashed out with a right hand doubled into a fist. Horne ducked under it, shook MacPherson once, then shoved him backwards. Bill fell down, got up fast and waded into Horne, fists flailing like whirlygigs. Horne nimbly sidestepped the man, stuck out a foot. MacPherson tripped, slid face down through the snow. Horne set himself, waited for the man to recover.

Bill stood up, his face puffed with rage and came at Horne again. Horne drew back a fist, rammed it straight into MacPherson's chin. Bill went down like a poleaxed steer. He didn't get up for several seconds. Panting, he struggled to his feet. He stood there, swaying slowly, blinking from the pain.

"That'll be enough, Mister Horne," said Faron. "The mon's distraught. He dinna mean what he said."

"Give it up, Bill," said Luke.

MacPherson's shoulders slumped and he sighed deeply, shook his head. Beaten, he walked back to his horse, slowly mounted it.

Horne retrieved his rifle as the men whispered among themselves.

"Look Horne," said Newcastle. The whispers died away like rustling leaves suddenly deserted by the wind. "I know you don't like us much, and maybe we don't hanker to your ways none much either, but we ask you in the name of Christian decency . . ."

Horne waved him to silence.

"Why don't you ask like men?" Horne thundered. "Might be none of this would have happened if some of you had stayed behind to look after your womenfolks instead of skylarking after game like a bunch of schoolboys. Well, the damage has been done, and I'll go after the Arapaho on my own hook. But don't expect anything and don't push me."

"On your terms?" Luke said it soft, shot MacPherson a hard look.

"On my terms."

"Done," said MacGregor, letting out a sigh of relief. "You'll have nae more trouble from us, Mister Horne."

Horne started to say something, held his tongue. He turned, then, strode toward his cabin. The men watched him go, then Luke kicked his horse in the flanks. The others rode behind him, like punished children.

It was the most talk any of them had ever heard from the laconic man, and the seeds of their suspicion and hatred of him were pushed deeper into the loam of their minds. Their values had been questioned, shattered. They had been made to feel guilty by Horne's stinging words. They had seen the broad gulf that stretched between them and Horne. They were all married men, and Horne a bachelor, strange in his ways. There was none among them who trusted him, or genuinely liked him. But, as Faron MacGregor had told them a few moments before, they would be eating his meat while he was gone, and if the truth be known, he was their only hope.

Horne rode past Caleb's trading post as the people assembled to watch him go.

Elizabeth Simmons was the only one who dared speak.

"Bring back my girls, Mister Horne," she pleaded. "Please!"

Horne did not reply.

They watched him ride up the trail until he was small and dark and then he disappeared over the ridge, leaving them alone with their thoughts, the terrible suspicions that had already begun to fester like a swelling boil in their minds.

CHAPTER 7

HORNE had his own reasons for going after Red Hawk. The Arapaho band had come into the valley like invaders. He knew they had never been there before. But, they knew how to find it, and that bothered him. He had said nothing to the men back there. It would just give them one more thing to worry about. Well, it was a thing to worry about. Red Hawk might come back some day and bring a hundred braves instead of six. Red Hawk had known about the settlement all right. And Horne knew damned well the Arapaho hadn't heard about it from him.

The pines threw shadows across the trail once Horne cleared the barren, windswept ridge. The bright sun set the snow adazzle and Horne couldn't look at the whiteness without going temporarily blind. In shadow, the snow had a pearly cast to it, and as the day bore on, the melt turned the windwept places to mud. He had no trouble following the tracks of the men and he saw where they had stopped, turned around. The thaw had revealed the pock marks left by their horses' hooves, little frozen castles and spires preserved by the cold and snowfall, uncovered now by the sun.

Red Hawk, too, had left a clear trail. His ponies had cut up the snow, churned it in with the dirt, left the tell-tale clumps along his path. Horne knew the tracking would become more difficult, but for now, he was content. The Arapaho had not hurried the first few hours after they left Sky Valley, but had taken the main trail over the mountains, riding in the lee of the storm below the southeastern slopes. That was where he would have holed up, too, Horne reasoned, and he began to scan the highlands, looking for caves, outcroppings, natural shelters.

Horne thought of what Simmons had told him about the Arapaho. They had been painted for war, yet they had not come to the valley as a war party. Likely, they had warred on Utes and got their feathers singed. If they had come after whites, that trading post, the Simmons cabin, even Simmons himself, and his woman, would not be there now. Red Hawk would have killed or captured every one of them and burned the structures to the ground. No, he had come there out of hunger, out of desperation. The Arapaho loved dog meat. Horne had eaten of it himself, but he had no taste for it. The point was that Red Hawk knew there was a white settlement there, a store where his braves could get whiskey, and he wouldn't pass up taking some young white women back to his camp. Red Hawk loved the women. He had a strong voice when he talked to men, but when he spoke to a woman his voice softened, and lowered to a husky whisper.

When he left Major Drips, the "Captain," as some called him, Horne had fled south to Santa Fe, to Taos, and then drifted north, following the natural lay of the land, the old buffalo trails, the antelope herds. He avoided people, but there was no trick to that. He seldom saw another white man, and when he smelled Indians, he got out of their way. He crossed a pass into Jefferson Territory, followed the Rio Grande up into the Rockies. He fished, hunted, traded for flour, coffee and beans whenever he felt the need. He liked being in country where he could ride free and not have to listen to the clatter of traps and chains, the grumbling of other men.

Horne had gotten his belly full of the white man's civilization, in St. Louis, Taos, Santa Fe, Independence. When he was but a boy, he did not know any better, but after living with the free trappers, and then seeing the men fight over territories, make deals with the big fur companies, he had wanted no more of it. He saw the end of the beaver, the finish of the free trapper, a death he could not fathom, a murder, maybe, that was an eternal scar on his soul. He had come into the wilderness alone, he told himself, he would go out the same way.

But he didn't count on running into the Utes up where the Rio Grande made its headwaters. He didn't figure on becoming a part of the Indian's way of life, either. He thought of the years that had gone by and the first time he had seen Red Hawk, the Arapaho. It seemed a long time ago, but as he trailed Red Hawk's band Horne could see the man in his mind, remember him that first time when the Utes had tried to kill him. Horne smiled wryly. He was green then, green to the ways of the Ute and the Arapaho. He had met up with the Cheyenne, the Blackfoot, the Kiowa and the Pawnee, and he wanted no part of them. But he was ignorant of the Utes and their territory when he made camp up above the Rio Grande on a little stream where there were still beaver, and no sign that any white man had ever stepped there.

He had plenty of staples in his larder and shot and powder enough to last him the summer. He planned to stay until just before the first snow, then ride down to milder climes. He had been camped there two days when he found deer sign and tracked a mule deer buck to the high country. While tracking the animal, he came across a single set of moccasin prints heading in the same direction.

The hackles rose on the back of Horne's neck. Some instinct clawed at him, told him to run, to get away from there as fast as he could. Curiosity swelled up in him and he pressed on.

He took each step with care, senses alert to any alien sound, any movement. The woods were quiet, filled with downed timber. Huge dead trees crisscrossed the forest floor. Game trails laced in and out, over and beyond the deadfalls in a bewildering maze. Horne followed the deer and moccasin tracks, sniffed the faint scents rising from the moist earth. He had learned to develop his sense of smell during his trapping days. A man who did not use tobacco, he discovered, and who took the time to examine and isolate different aromas, could detect the presence of game or man. Each creature left a scent, whether it be the rutting bull elk, the beaver, the doe in heat, the sweating white man or the painted Indian.

The scent of the mule deer was not strong yet, so Horne knew the animal had not sighted or smelled him. But the Indian scent was strong, a mixture of grease and squaw-wood smoke mingled with other aromas he could not define. He climbed over a log that the deer had jumped, and slipped on the mossy loam, half-slid over the rough bark to one knee.

He heard the odd sound, could not, at first, tell what it was. Then he heard the faint thrum of the bowstring as it snapped. Horne threw himself headlong onto the ground, and heard the rippling whifflesong of the arrow as it passed a few inches over him. *Whip-o, whop-o, whip-whop,* until the shaft struck the log with a *crack.*

Horne rolled, his possibles pouch flopping and rattling like tin dishes in a wagon. He hoped he hadn't spilled the powder out his pan as he struggled to bring his Hawken to bear on the man who had shot at him. The lock caught on the fringed buckskin of his sleeves, his possibles bag got tangled up with his powder horns. Horne crawled ahead, set up behind another fallen tree, his heart throbbing in his throat, the fear in him slicking his palms, turning his fingers to wood. He cursed, jerked the rifle free of the fringe, quickly checked the pan. The powder was there, still dry, he hoped. He closed the frizzen, listened.

He peered over the top of the dead pine, saw the Indian draw his short bow. The arrow seemed to come at him in slow motion, yet grow larger faster than he could duck in time to avoid it. But duck he did, and the shaft caromed off the log. He saw its vanes flash in the sun before it arced into the high branches of a tall pine. Horne cocked his rifle and laid it across the pine. He brought the sights into alignment on the Indian as the man drew another arrow from his quiver, nocked it. Horne fired, and a cloud of white smoke and a spray of orange flame burst from the muzzle. The smoke obscured the Indian and provided Horne with cover, as well.

Horne grabbed the big powder horn, threw the butt of his rifle across his boot moccasin. He had no time to measure, but poured powder down the smoking muzzle until he figured he had around a hundred grains. He reached into his possibles pouch and found a ball and a piece of greased patching. He set the ball on the patch, rammed it partway down the barrel with his short starter. Quickly, he jerked the ramrod free, hurled it down the barrel. He jammed the rod against the tree, seating the ball and patch over the powder. He crawled along the log on his butt, untangled the small powder horn, and after flipping the frizzen back, shook fine powder into the pan. He flipped the frizzen back over the pan and got his feet under him. He waddled to the end of the log, circled it and crouching, crossed to a tree. He stood up, breathing hard. He hefted the rifle into a position where he could bring it to his shoulder.

He leaned around the tree, watched the last of the smoke break into wisps, waft away like spider silk on the gentle drafts of forest zephyrs. The Indian was down on his knees, clutching his belly. Blood oozed between his fingers. Horne froze when he saw another Indian a few yards away, hunched over, his bow half drawn, a nocked arrow pointing at the spot where Horne had fired his rifle.

Horne eased his rifle up slowly to his shoulder, backed away from the tree so that the muzzle didn't jut out. He laid the barrel against the tree, squeezed the trigger slightly, cocked the hammer back soundlessly. He found the target over the blade front sight, tilted his rifle so that the rear buckhorn fell into line. He squeezed the trigger, just as the Indian turned toward him. The explosion was deafening, and the kick of the rifle butt pounded Horne's shoulder, knocked him backwards, off-balance. He heard a wild scream, the *swish-thud* of footsteps running toward him. A third Indian bounded toward him like something out of Hell. Horne laid down his Hawken, pulled his hatchet from his belt with his left hand, his knife with his right.

A small, moon-faced Indian, flat nosed, with high, apple-rounded cheekbones, charged through the smoke, yelling his war cry. The brave held a stone warclub in his hand, wore only a breechclout and moccasins. Horne drew back his left arm, but the brave barreled into him before he could throw. Horne went down, with a clawing panther on his chest. The Indian tried to brain him with his club as Horne squirmed, tried to get the flailing madman off his torso. He rolled, kicked, stabbed with his knife. The Indian was like a wood-tick. He wouldn't shake loose. The club grazed Horne's shoulder, slammed into the ground, buried two inches in the soft earth.

Horne brought his knife up in a slow arc, rammed it into the Indian's neck. He heard the blade slide across the man's spine as blood gushed from the artery into Horne's eyes. The Indian gurgled, went limp. Blinded, Horne scrambled away, wiped a buckskinned sleeve across his eyes. The Indian thrashed around for a few seconds like a beheaded chicken, then kicked twice, reflexively, and lay still. A small lake of blood pooled under the dead man's shoulder. Horne staggered away, breathless, turned his head in all directions as he half-crouched, expecting another attack.

That's when he saw still another Indian, standing there, naked, his hands bound behind him with the same horsehair rope that encircled his neck, his skin a mass of ugly welts, his cheek laid open where a knife had cut through to the bone. Horne's hand tightened around the blood-slick handle of his blade.

This Indian appeared to be from a different tribe than the other three. He was leaner, his features sharper, his black hair longer, and he showed no fear as Horne approached him warily, his knife and hatchet at the ready. The first Indian that Horne had shot, swayed on his knees, still alive, gutshot, less than ten yards from where the bound prisoner stood. The second Indian was stone dead, one side of his skull blown out by the flattened .54 caliber ball that must have had almost 200 grains of black powder pushing it. Horne's shoulder still ached.

Horne drove the blade into the wounded Indian's heart and the man toppled over, quivering in his death throes. Horne looked at the prisoner, looked straight into his eyes. The man smiled at him. Horne wondered whether he should kill him and be on his way. He stood there for a long time, mulling it over in his mind.

Horne thought about that moment now, as he began ascending the steep slope, following the roiled snow track, his senses attuned to the woodsounds, ignoring the thrash of his horse's hooves as they flattened melting snow.

"Maybe I should have kilt that red bastard then," he muttered under his breath. The words sounded familiar to him, for he had uttered them many times before.

Horne cursed the wasted time. He cursed Red Hawk and every Arapaho man, woman and child he had ever known. He looked down at the ruins of Red Hawk's storm camp with mixed emotions. He had found the place where the wily brave had spent the night before, but he hadn't just picked any place and he hadn't ridden to it straight in. Instead the Arapaho had gone in a circle and doubled back. The camp was high above the trail, a rock ledge protected by stunted juniper, pine and cedar.

"So, Red Hawk," said Horne, "you found you a place where the white owl couldn't find you." The Arapaho called a snow storm by that name and Horne had always thought it was good enough. Every man-jack of them put names and breath to things that most white men never paid much attention to. There was garbage and feces strewn along the ledge, depressions where they had spread their blankets. He found the tracks of the white women, too, knew they were still alive. He looked down at his backtrail, let out a ragged sigh. If the men from the valley had come up that trail on Red Hawk's heels they would have been cut to pieces.

The Arapaho had tethered their ponies just below the ledge, in a sheltered grove of blue spruce and small firs. From the sign, they had flushed a covey of grouse when they rode in. They had made a single track walking up to the ledge and the last man, he knew, had almost brushed that away. They were like wolves in winter, Horne thought. They disappeared into thin air. You couldn't see them, but they were there.

He gave Tony a rest, built a small fire out of squaw-wood. The small dead branches wrested from the lower trunk of pines made a quick blazing fire. He heated some snow to save his water, put some coffee grounds and venison chunks in the pot. He let the concoction boil for a good ten minutes while he warmed his hands and boots. He filled his tin cup, drank noisily, munched on the hot venison. He wiped out the pot and cup with snow, repacked them in his canvas saddle bags. He checked the load in his rifle, mounted Tony and took up the trail again. He wished he could see into Red Hawk's mind, know where he was going. But that was something he had never been able to do.

Horne could never explain what it was about Red Hawk that made him cut his bonds. But afterwards, he was damned glad he had turned the Arapaho loose. Horne couldn't speak his language, but Red Hawk told him in hand sign something he would never forget.

Those were Ute Indians Horne had killed. A scouting party that had captured Red Hawk and were on their way back to camp. Red Hawk showed Horne where the camp was—not far from where they stood; it was full of the

Arapaho's and the white man's natural enemies, more than a hundred warriors who would soon come looking for the three Utes Horne had killed.

Red Hawk talked Horne out of his knife. Horne wondered why he had allowed the Indian to do that, but in retrospect, he guessed he knew all along that he and this man were meant to be friends. He stood by, with only his hatchet for protection, while Red Hawk took the Ute scalps. Then, he stripped a breechclout from one of the dead men for himself and told Horne to follow him, Horne retrieved his rifle, reloaded it on the run, and they made tracks to where Horne had his pony. He and Red Hawk rode north, out of the country where the Ute summered, and gradually Horne learned to speak the Arapaho tongue. He taught Red Hawk some English and between them, they could pretty much say what was on their minds.

At one point in their flight, Red Hawk had taken Horne to the rimrock, above timberline, and showed him one of the huge Ute camps. He learned that the Ute did not camp near running water, and they always picked high, open ground, where their scouts could see for miles in every direction. Yet, they stayed close to trees, where the people could scatter and hide when trouble came. Horne began to harbor a deep and abiding respect for the Ute, but he knew that the feeling wasn't mutual.

Horne learned that Red Hawk had lived twenty winters and had been separated from a hunting party when the Utes captured him. Red Hawk's horse had been bitten by a rattlesnake, had bolted and run off, leaving the Arapaho afoot. When Red Hawk fell from his horse, he broke his bow. The Utes had run him down and captured him.

Red Hawk rode behind Horne, directed him to an Arapaho camp on the prairie. The lodges were set in the shape of a horseshoe, and when they rode in, the people all came out to see why Red hawk was riding with a white man on a white man's horse.

"We thought you were dead," said Red Hawk's friends. "Why are you with a white man?"

"This man has white skin," said Red Hawk. "But he will live as an Arapaho. He will learn our ways, live in our lodges."

"You will never teach a white man to live as an Arapaho," said Iron Knife.

"I will teach this one."

"What do you call him?"

"He killed three Ute braves. They tried to kill him. They shot arrows at him and they tried to strike him with a war club. He killed them with his fire-striking stick. He was like the gray wolf. He moved like a shadow and the Ute could not kill him."

"We will call him Gray Wolf, then," said Crow Caller.

The Indians wanted to see his rifle and they inspected the .54 caliber Hawken at length. "It does not shoot with the little shining caps," observed Red Hawk. In time, Horne was able to explain that he had bought the rifle from a gunsmith named Jake Hawken in St. Louis and had it made with a flintlock especially for him. Most of the men he trapped with used percussion caps, but they were the ones who always got them wet or used them up. "If a man uses flint, he can always explode his powder," said Horne.

He lived with the Arapaho for a time, and learned their ways and their language. Red Hawk became his friend, and the friendship was strong. Yet later when they became enemies, the hatred was even stronger than the friendship.

Horne knew that Red Hawk and his band would head for their camp, but not in a direct way. At this time of year, the various bands would be thinking of the prairie, the flat lands east of the Rockies. Yet, many of them were probably still in the mountains, hunting Utes and game. He knew some of their favorite places, but they had been driven out of some of these over the years.

The trail he followed now was the one the Arapaho had

ridden in on, but where had they been? Were there Utes somewhere in these mountains? If so, Horne knew the Arapaho would have to find a way out. He still believed that Red Hawk had led a war party against the Utes, for he hated them more than whites. And, if the Utes had tracked Red Hawk, they could be waiting for the Arapaho's return.

The dazzling snow blinded Horne and he cut a piece of leather from his shirt, cut slits in it and holes for two pieces of fringe he sliced from his sleeve. He wore the leather like a mask over his eyes, and the slits helped to keep him from going blind.

Late in the afternoon, Tony began to tire, and Horne knew he would have to find a place to camp for the night. The temperature dropped sharply as he descended into a steep, long canyon, the snow in the shadows already crusted. Tony's hooves broke through deep drifts and ice slashed at his fetlocks.

The wind blew hard in the canyon, and Horne knew he would have to strike for the other side, get out of the deep drifts, away from places where the snow could slide and bury him until spring. He rode on slowly, letting Tony pick his way, holding him to the tracks that were more visible now, dark holes where other ponies had broken through. He saw an occasional fleck of blood and knew that Red Hawk was faring worse than he.

Horne crossed the deepest part of the canyon, and flushed a lone grouse that spooked Tony. The horse reared up, the cinch loosened, and the saddle slid sideways. Horne shifted his weight and held onto the animal's mane, righted the saddle, but had to dismount after he wrestled Tony to a halt. He tightened the cinch on his Indian saddle, what the trappers called a "prairie chicken snare saddle." He had made it himself, using the fork from a tree for the pommel and bending a limb for the cantle. He covered it with rawhide and sewed on a buffalo hide for the soft seat. It was useable, lighter in weight than the Spanish saddles favored by many he had trapped with a dozen years back.

He remounted, rode on toward the opposite slope, still following the tracks of the Arapaho. In the thick timber, the tracks separated, not gradually, but all at once. Horne cursed and a plume of steam jetted from his mouth.

The eastern slope filled with shadows as the sun fell away behind the ridge. The Indians had scattered like quail here, and Horne could almost hear Red Hawk laughing. He realized that, somewhere along the bottom of the canyon, Red Hawk had cut a new trail. A hard trail. Now, he had split the band up, and if he knew his man, the Arapaho would not have his braves join back up for a long stretch of distance. Likely, he would do it gradually, leaving maybe one or two men to keep up the deception.

Horne knew he would have to be careful from now on. At least one brave would double back, check the backtrail. He would find Horne's tracks, report to Red Hawk. Beyond that, Horne knew he must pick a track to follow and that was the hardest part.

If he made a mistake, he would lose any gains he had made. If he took after the wrong track, he could lose more than time.

The shadows deepened and Horne rode in a circle to check the tracks one last time before making a decision. In the tall timber, he was blind. He could not see the ridge, nor assess the lay of the land.

"Red Hawk, you sonofabitch," he muttered. "I should have killed you when I first laid eyes on you."

CHAPTER 8

HORNE looked for double sets of tracks. He knew there would have to be at least three. Red Hawk would not leave the woman unguarded. "Look for the woman," he laughed wryly. It was an old maxim handed down by some mistrusting man. If there was trouble, a woman was usually behind it. Horne widened his circle, knowing he was wasting valuable time. If he was to survive the night, he must make a warm camp and do it quick. The dark was on him, and the cold drove into him through the sheepskin coat until his teeth clattered like rattling dice in a cup.

He found one set of double tracks, turned Tony in a tight formation to trample the spot around them. If the weather held, and it didn't snow, he could easily find this place in the morning. He rode for a level spot, looked for bare places under the spruce where he might hole up for the night, built a small fire to keep himself warm. He pulled his tomahawk from his belt, cut blazes on the pines as he rode through the gathering darkness.

He climbed higher, switched back to take the slope at an angle, avoid tiring Tony any more than was necessary. The horse was good on a trail, any trail, but there was no trail here and the way was strewn with obstacles: loose rocks, boulders, downed timber. Something flashing white caught Horne's eye. He hauled in on the reins, froze. The object danced near a tree fifty yards ahead of him. He watched it long enough to know that it was not alive. "Too early for snowy owl," he muttered, but the hairs on the back of his neck bristled as if spiders had hatched there.

Carefully, he guided Tony to the fluttering object, saw that it was a piece of cloth. It dangled on the end of a spruce bough. He leaned over, snatched it away, brought it up to his face. He smelled it, felt it. In the dark, he could not make out details, but an anger started to boil in him. The material was not Arapaho, but something belonging to a white man—or a woman. Horne's jaw tightened in sudden anger. He stuffed the piece of cloth in his pocket. Whatever it was, it would keep until morning.

Horne found a level spot, protected on three sides. A stand of spruce grew above a rock outcropping. He stripped Tony of his saddle, hobbled him and gave him a hatful of precious grain, slipped a halter over his head in place of a bridle. Quickly, Horne cut spruce boughs for a wind shelter, gathered squaw–wood for a fire. He kicked snow loose from rotten, aged branches, carried them back to his camp. He struck a sulphur match and the squaw–wood caught like tinder. He spread out his bedroll atop spruce boughs placed under the living branches of the tree he had selected for his roof. He kept the fire small, fed it wet dead branches, boiled water for his horse, some for himself.

He was taking a chance, he knew, making a camp like this, but he figured Red Hawk would be putting miles between him and Sky Valley. The tracks were more than a day old here, and by morning they would be even older. No, the Arapaho would not send a scout down the backtrail this soon. Tomorrow maybe, or the next. But Red Hawk acted as if he knew he would be followed, and maybe he wanted to see the faces of the men who came after him. That was Red Hawk's way. He was arrogant, proud, opinionated, and just plain mean.

Horne ate sparingly, wiped his rifle dry and checked the hammer's setscrew. This was the third lock he had put on the Hawken since Jake made the first one for him. Well, old Jake was dead now, since '49, though he'd heard Sam was still alive, but hadn't much heart for the business anymore. They made good percussion rifles, all right, and yet Horne had never regretted having Jake put flint on one of his half-stock 40-inchers. It had been a hell of a job of cutting and fitting the lock, but Jake, as usual, did a perfect job. The rifle, with its egg-lock that had a waterproof pan, roller-mounted frizzen, swan-neck hammer and fly in the tumbler, had served Horne well. Now, he had gotten used to the caplock, with its faster ignition. But he missed the old puff and spark of that first flinter, the delayed *whuff* before the powder charge exploded.

When he had set out from St. Louis with Major Drips, the rifle had been Horne's most costly possession. He was glad to be rid of the heavy Lancaster he had carried all the way from Kentucky, however, and was able to make up part of the cost of the Hawken by selling the old gun to another green trapper. Horne chuckled when he thought of it. Drips carried a percussion Hawken and so did some of the other men, and they ragged him about how slow the flinter ignited. But Horne outshot them all at rendezvous and when they funned in winter camps, so they finally quit casting jibes and let him be.

He thought of the men who had been his friends back then. Jess Coons, he had known longer than any. Jess had told him about this country south of the Medicine Bows. Jess would laugh now to know that Horne had lived with the Arapaho. Coons had lived with the Cheyenne, talked about their friends, the Arapaho. Horne wondered if Jess had died, or gone back to the Medicine Bow mountains. There was Johnny Sanderson, too, and Lem Pickard, but they might even be dead by this time. The mountains were hard on a man, and in Lakota and Cheyenne country, they could shorten a man's life by many winters. Horne had not come this way in a long while because he did not know if his old friends would ever forgive him or want to see him again. But it looked like Red Hawk was going to run for the Medicine Bows unless Horne could catch up with him first.

Maybe things would have turned out different, he

thought, if he had not. . . . He wiped the bad thoughts from his mind, but the bitterness, the anger at himself remained.

Horne squatted by the fire, took the piece of cloth from his coat pocket, held it up to the light. He turned it around, spread the garment with his fingers. Bloomers. There were bloodstains on them, primarily at the crotch, but scattered, front and back.

Horne crumpled up the bloodied underpants and tossed them angrily into the fire. With cold hard eyes, he watched them burn. The flames devoured the white cloth, turned the bloomers black, licked them to ashes.

He closed his eyes for a moment as the memories of another time flooded back into his mind. He opened them again, looked past the fire, into the night, but the images would not go away. "Damn," he said, in a soft whisper.

They called her Sleeping Water and Horne lost his heart to her during his third year with the Arapaho. He did not know all of the Arapaho customs then, but he had listened to the long stories told by the tribe historian and medicine man, Weasel–Bear, even the four-night-long story of the creation of the world and the two tribes of men by *Nihansa,* the creator.

Sleeping Water was a Cheyenne girl, and when she came to the tribe with her new Arapaho family she had only recently gone through puberty. Horne looked at her, and her beauty was such that she caught his heart in her hands. She had light skin, like the color of the claybank horse he rode then, and her hair, dark as lampblack, shone in the sun like the glistening raven's wing. Her eyes were like the ripe currant berries that grew on the autumn hillsides, black and shiny, wide ovals, close-set like doe's eyes. Her nose was very beautiful, straight and smooth, slightly hooked like the hawk's beak. Her lips were full and delicately pronounced. They seemed always to be slightly aquiver with an unspoken promise. When she smiled, she made Horne glow inside, filled his loins with heat, made his stones ache for her. In her presence, however, he was struck dumb. When she walked by him, all of his confidence evaporated and he turned into a walleyed dolt. When he looked at her lithe figure, sheathed becomingly in soft white elkskin, his lust boiled with a volcanic intensity, but when he opened his mouth to speak, no words would come out. When she smiled that wise and mysterious smile at him, he could only wrinkle up his face until he was sure he looked like an addled dunce.

Sleeping Water was the woman who, when she touched him, made him feel as if she was squeezing his heart in her hands. She spoke as little of the Arapaho tongue as he, and he spoke no Cheyenne. It came to both of them, as their love for one another ripened, that they were both prisoners, not only of the tribe, but of their own hearts.

She was adopted by two old people, Found–in–Grass and Buffalo Woman. Buffalo Woman did not like Sleeping Water because she was too pretty. Found–in–Grass did not like her because his wife would kick him everytime he looked at the young woman. Horne saw this, and saw too, that the young men were starting to court her. He had seen them court other girls, and he asked Found–in–Grass if he might join the men who came to her lodge and covered their faces with blankets.

Found–in–Grass thought it would be a great joke if the white Arapaho married his adopted daughter. He gave his permission, although it was not necessary. Horne became one of the men who stood at Sleeping Water's lodge, waiting for her to come out. Red Hawk wanted her too, and he made it difficult for Horne.

But Horne was the most persistent, the most love-struck. When the young men left on hunting parties, he would stay behind, wrap himself in a robe and wait for her to fetch water or wood. When she returned, he threw his arms and the blanket around her, drew her close to him and talked, sometimes for an hour or two. Horne talked to her in broken

Arapaho and in English, and she always laughed and never pushed him away as she did Red Hawk and the other men.

Weasel–Bear, who liked Horne, called him to his *tipi* one day. They sat and smoked the pipe after offering the tobacco to the four directions and to the spirits.

"You want this woman Sleeping Water much."

"Yes," said Horne.

"I will make you a flute. Learn to play it. You must also kill a deer and make a deer-tail lure that will capture her heart. I will tell you how to do this. She will want you to be her husband after that. I will give you spruce gum to chew and that will attract her."

"Why do you do this for me?" asked Horne.

"Found–in–Grass filled his pipe and came to me. Red Hawk took the wristlet of Sleeping Water yesterday. She did not want him to have it. Found–in–Grass did not want him to have it. She did not give Red Hawk the bone ring she wears on her finger. Her father went to Red Hawk and took back the wristlet. Now Red Hawk is angry. Found–in–Grass wants you as a son-in-law, but you must make Sleeping Water give you her ring. You must make a bone ring and give it to her if she gives you her ring."

Horne knew that she wore a ring. She had made it herself, soaking it in boiling water. Red Hawk made a similar ring, too, and he wore that when he was courting Sleeping Water.

"I will do these things," said Horne. "I want Sleeping Water to be my wife."

"Good. Go kill the white-tailed deer and I will make you a flute and teach you how to play it. It will have a special power. When Sleeping Water hears you play it, she will come out of her lodge."

Horne went off alone to kill the white-tailed deer. When he returned, he tied his medicine to the deer tail, wore it over his shoulder. He learned to play the flute as Weasel–Bear had instructed him. He would begin to play some distance from Sleeping Water's lodge and by the time he reached it, she would be outside, waiting for him. They rubbed noses and kissed under Horne's blanket and talked of everything but their love for one another. One day, he took her wristlet. She did not ask for it back.

When she was with the other young girls, Horne wore the deer's tail over his shoulder. He chewed the spruce gum. He walked close to her on the windward side so she could smell the deer's tail. She broke away from the other girls one day, more than a year after he had starting courting her, and walked boldly up to him.

"Why don't you tell me what you want?" she said.

"I want you."

"What?"

"I want to marry you, Sleeping Water."

"Are you telling the truth? If you are, Gray Wolf, take my ring." She thrust out her hand. Horne looked at the ring. He was quivering inside. He took the ring. He put it on his finger.

"I want to marry you, too, Gray Wolf," she said.

"Are you telling me the truth?" he asked. "If you are, Sleeping Water, you will have to take my ring."

He held out his hand. She smiled at him and took his ring, put it on her finger. Horne wanted to let out a whoop, but he quelled the impulse.

They were as good as married, but Horne knew he had to wait for some time to see if she sent his ring back to him. When she did not, Horne sent two horses to her father with a messenger. The messenger told Found–in–Grass that, "Gray Wolf, the white Arapaho, wishes to marry your daughter, Sleeping Water." The messenger did not wait for an answer, but went away.

Horne's stomach roiled all that day as the horses stood outside the lodge. Found–in–Grass had twenty-four hours to accept or reject Horne's offer. Horne wondered how he could last the night if the old man didn't decide that day.

Finally, as the sun was setting, Found–in–Grass came out of his lodge and took the horses to his pasture.

Horne went to the lodge and called out for Sleeping Water. "Will you come with me now?" he asked.

"Yes. I have my things. Do you have a lodge for me?"

"I have a new lodge for you," he said. "You will have to put it up."

"I will put it up."

Horne took her hand and they walked away from her lodge. Buffalo Woman called out that it was good riddance, and slammed the door flap closed so hard that it sounded like a rifle shot.

The morning broke cold and clear. Horne's blankets were warm around his body, but the edges were frozen to the ground. He knew this would be the last night he would sleep in such comfort as long as he was in the mountains. He hoped to gain on Red Hawk this day, but he also knew that the closer he got to the Arapaho, the more dangerous his mission would become.

Horne stirred the coals, put fresh wood on them to make a fire. He made coffee, swallowed hardtack and jerky to fill the empty hole in his belly. He rubbed Tony down good with spruce needles, saddled him, and loaded his bedroll and gear for the day's ride. Fifteen minutes later, he picked up the trail and dismounted to cinch up again.

"Tony," he said, "you swelled up on me. You know better'n that." He loosened the cinch, gave it a quick jerk. Tony puffed his belly up. Horne slapped the horse's belly with the backside of his hand. Tony let out his breath, slacked up, and Horne jerked the cinch tight. "You don't want to drop me off a damned cliff, do you boy?" Tony snorted, but he was cinched up. The flat of Horne's hand just barely slid between the cinch and hide.

Horne followed a set of tracks made by two unshod ponies. They wound through the timber, but angled upslope gradually. The tracks were so close together, Horne figured one of the women must be with a lone brave. If his hunch was correct, the tracks would join up with the others, somewhere higher up.

He watched the sky carefully. The winds began stirring, circling, sniffing like a wolf at his coat. The high clouds began to thin and spread out, blow away in wisps until they resembled mare's tails—a sure sign that another storm was working its way into the Rockies.

The tracks doubled back, still climbing at an angle, and when he topped the mountain, these were joined by another two sets of tracks. The ride had taken him the better part of three hours.

It took another two hours before he found where the Arapahos had come back together. Now, he had a wide swath of tracks to follow, and they traversed a high meadow, veered to the northeast.

After he reached the timber, the tracks turned back to the northwest, but he almost missed it in the brushy draw where the tracks led. The snow was mangled here, churned up and Horne knew why. It was rocky in there, and the brush thick, rising out of the snow in a bramble thicket of bare but sturdy limbs that tore at his boots and trousers. Tony floundered in the drifts, wobbled off of buried stones. Horne dismounted. He didn't want Tony to break a leg in there.

He led the horse out of the pocket and was about to climb back into the saddle when he saw what he wasn't supposed to see. He couldn't explain it, but something was wrong with the tracks. They were evenly spaced, as if Red Hawk had put the horses in a formation. Side by side, the Indians and their captives had ridden downslope, over fallen timber, through open places.

"Now, I wonder why he did that?" Horne said to himself.

He dismounted once again and started counting tracks.

Then, he knew. There was one pony short in the count.

Somewhere, back where he had ridden out of that craggy draw, he figured, Red Hawk had sent out his first scout. Rather, he had just dropped the man off and Horne figured out how he had done it.

While the others were going ahead, side by side, this scout had sidestepped his pony and backed up the churned snow in the pocket. Horne didn't need to go back there. He knew he'd find a snowslide above it that wiped out the pony's tracks where the brave had climbed the slope.

The hackles bristled on the back of Horne's neck. He froze, listened to the prowling wind, the silent spaces that echoed hollow in between the slicing gusts. Had he come too far? Not far enough? He looked up into the timber and it was like looking down the main street of a ghost town. There was no movement, no sound except the wind, and yet he knew there was somebody there.

When the wind picked up again, he could almost hear the warcry of his attacker, the keening trill of an Arapaho brave as he rode down on him swinging his tomahawk in circles over his head.

But it was only the wind. Horne was almost sure of that. Still, his scalp began to prickle and the cold crept inside his coat and made him shiver.

He was about to step back into the saddle when he heard it.

A branch cracked, and the sound of it echoed through the timber like a bullwhip.

The wind? Horne did not know. An elk, maybe.

He slid his Hawken free of its scabbard, checked the nipple to see if the cap was down tight. He sucked under Tony's belly, hunched over still lower as he stepped carefully toward a thick pine.

He heard more sound, hooves crashing through snow, the slap and creak of leather as a horse came toward him. He looked around the tree, saw a dim shape growing larger. His senses flared with warning. Something was wrong, but he couldn't figure it out as his blood pumped hot, and the cold in him went away, the chillbumps subsided on his arms and his hair stopped tingling. Almost too late, he heard the other, nearly imperceptible, sound. This, he knew, was the sound of death itself.

He had only a single shrinking moment to make a decision.

CHAPTER 9

HORNE knew what to do. He knew how to decipher the sounds. He knew what his eyes told him. He knew how to trust his ears. Yet it took every effort of his will to turn away from the galloping pony and the brave hugging its side, his bow pulled to full draw. He forced himself in the dwindling fraction of that moment to turn his back on the more distant brave and bring the Hawken to his shoulder while he sought the other Arapaho with his eyes and ears.

He shut out the sound of the hooves crunching through crusted snow and brought all his senses to bear on the other sound, the soft pad of moccasins coming toward him as relentless as the stalk of a painter. He eased toward the tree, protection for his back, and he crouched low, feeling the pressure of seconds splitting up into fractions and the fractions falling through a hole in time like grains of fine sand through an hourglass.

Horne cocked the Hawken as he brought it to his shoulder. He heard the comforting click as the sear engaged, locked in. He pulled the set-trigger back, inched his finger forward to curl around the front trigger. He had only to cough now, and the rifle would fire.

Wood Jumper came at him, his war ax held high, a ghostly white figure, nearly invisible against the blinding glaze of the sunstruck snow. The brave let out a terrible cry of victory as Horne picked him up in his sights.

The Arapaho closed the yardage, bounding toward Horne in long, ground-eating leaps, a lethal dancer driving in for the kill. Horne almost hated to shoot, but as Wood Jumper came down and drew his arm back for the throw, the mountain man ticked the front trigger and rocked backward against the tree as the powder in the barrel exploded. A hundred grains of black powder rocketed the .54 caliber lead ball unerringly towards its target. A cloud of white smoke billowed from the muzzle, obscuring Wood Jumper. The blowback peppered Horne's cheek, scorched a corner of his eye.

He whirled, then, flipped the rifle so that he gripped it by its hot barrel. He took a half-step away from the tree, rested the stock of his rifle on his shoulder as the crunching hoofbeats thundered in his ears. Seven Stars, the other brave, fired the arrow straight at Horne, jerked the braided horsehair reins over hard to turn the pony. The arrow wiffed a scant two inches above Horne's head, struck a pine with a blunt thud, twanged like a broken piano string.

Horne stood up full length, stepped away from the tree and swung the Hawken as the Indian pony slurred the snow in a violent skid. The buttplate caught Seven Stars just below the knee with bone-crunching force.

Snow sprayed up, splatted Horne as the skidding pony made the turn. Seven Stars howled in pain, wobbled, his leg's grip broken by the blow from the rifle.

His breath coming hard now, burning his lungs, Horne slammed the rifle butt down into the snow. He poured powder down the barrel, measuring by instinct. He opened his patchbox, slid out a greased piece of cloth he had precut into a square. He pulled a ball from his possibles bag and buried it in the patch as he clawed for his short starter. He deftly put the patch and ball atop the muzzle opening, pushed the ball in with the shorter peg, then rammed it further down with the longer one. He pulled the ramrod from under the barrel and dropped it down the barrel. He turned, jammed the rod hard against the pine tree to seat the ball. He jerked the rod free, let it fall to the snow and he placed the leather capper he wore around his neck over the nipple. The cap caught and Horne pushed it down tight with his thumb.

Seven Stars brought his pony under control, danced him through the trees, swung the animal around. He reined to a halt sixty yards away. Horne stood there, holding the Hawken across his chest, ready to shoulder in an instant.

"I know you, Seven Stars," he said, in Arapaho. "I have killed Wood Jumper." Horne knew it was so.

Seven Stars wore no expression on his painted face. His eyes did not blink. He did not nock another arrow. From his position in the trees, he could jump the pony into cover before Horne could cock and fire. Just the same, Horne's thumb eased up over the crosshatching on the top of the iron hammer.

Seven Stars made sign with his hands. Horne watched, translating the definite hand movements in his mind.

Seven Stars knows you Gray Wolf. The White Arapaho who lived with our people. You have killed Wood Jumper. I know this. My heart is on the ground. I will not kill you now. I am not afraid of Gray Wolf. You have a thunderstick. Seven Stars has a bow and a few arrows. Maybe we will fight again.

"Take Wood Jumper with you," Horne said, choosing the Arapaho words carefully. "Bury him with honor. Tell Red Hawk I come. I will take the white women from him. The white women do not belong to Red Hawk." The smoke from his breath blew into shreds as the wind gusted.

Seven Stars, his scalplock ruffled by vagrant zephyrs, replied with his hands speaking for him. *Red Hawk does not know Gray Wolf walks on his trail. Gray Wolf was once the brother to Red Hawk. This was many snows behind us. Red Hawk would welcome you to his lodge again as his brother. You come with me and we will tell him you do not turn your face against him anymore.*

Horne felt the anger seethe in him. Seven Stars had grown some, had filled out his muscles. Maybe he had some scalps. But he had not grown a new brain for himself. He was a pony boy and a sneak when Horne had lived with the tribe, and Horne was sure he had not changed. He was never to be trusted. He stole and groveled for mercy whenever he was caught. It was difficult to think of Seven Stars as a warrior now, but Horne knew he was as deadly as any Arapaho. He respected them as a fighting people, but their time had run out with the thinning of the buffalo herds.

"I turn my face against Red Hawk. You tell him this. You tell him, I do not take Wood Jumper's hair for my belt. You tell him to leave the white women at the cradle in the mountains below that place where the snow stays until the moon of the horses getting fat. Then Gray Wolf will not put his moccasins on Red Hawk's trail anymore."

"Hounh!" barked Seven Stars. "I will do this, white man," he spat in his people's tongue. "I will take the dead body of Wood Jumper to Red Hawk."

"Do it, then, you sonofabitch," Horne said in English. He brought his rifle down to show Seven Stars that he would not harm him. He picked up his ramrod, shoved it angrily back under the barrel of the Hawken. He mounted his horse, waited as Seven Stars rode slowly past him.

Horne watched as Seven Stars dismounted, stooped to pick up the limp, snow–flocked body of Wood Jumper. The snow beneath the slain warrior was stained with blood, already freezing into crystals. Seven Stars lashed the body to his saddle, then picked up Wood Jumper's tomahawk and tucked it in his sash.

Seven Stars climbed up behind the low cantle of his saddle, made strong like the saddles of Sante Fe, with wood and leather. He rodé up close to Horne, looked him in the eyes.

He made sign with his hands. *There is snow in the sky now. The snow will come down like a blanket. My tracks will be like footprints on water, like words written in smoke.*

"Gray Wolf knows this is so. Gray Wolf will track Red Hawk, even if his footprints are on water, even if his tracks are like words written in smoke."

The two men spoke no more. Seven Stars rode off through the trees, climbing to the ridge above the trail where Red Hawk had gone. Horne knew it was no use to track the brave. He would backtrack and circle for days, weeks, if necessary, and get no closer to Red Hawk than he was now until he was sure Horne was not following him.

A great silence settled in the forest as the wind died down and the sky scudded over with high thick clouds that were gray as dead moss. Soon, Horne knew, the storm would come and he would lose the track as Seven Stars had said.

From then on, he knew, he would have to ride blind and try to think like an Arapaho. Once, that had been easy, because he had been one of them. If Sleeping Water had not died, he might still be with them. A white Arapaho. An outcast from his own kind. Would any of this have happened then? Would he have followed Red Hawk's path, no matter where it led?

Horne picked up the tracks again, kicked Tony in the flanks. He looked up at the skyline, felt the awesome emptiness of the big country around him, within him. He was an outcast, even so. Maybe he always had been. Maybe, he mused, he always would be.

CHAPTER 10

HORNE knew it was foolhardy to run Tony or work him too hard. If the horse sweated, the sweat would freeze in the knifing wind. The gallop had helped clear Horne's head and perhaps he had gained some lost ground. The tracks grew faint now as he rode into the teeth of the north wind, felt the portent of the coming storm in its probing gusts. Horne could not look at the sky anymore. It weighed down on him, a depressing, suffocating gray presence. Red Hawk could read the signs better than he, and Horne knew, with a sinking feeling of premonition, where the Arapaho was heading, where the tracks would peter out.

Yet the knowledge of Red Hawk's intent only served to harden Horne's resolve. The tracks now headed toward timberline and the barren, windswept eastern slopes that had somehow missed being in the path of that first storm. They would not escape this second one as it drifted down from the north, gathering strength, turning killer with every icy blast of wind.

He turned up the collar of his sheepskin coat, buried his face in the wool, breathed back inside it to preserve his body's heat. Still, the cold searched his exposed flesh with gelid fingers, plundered the warmth in his hands and feet as he climbed higher into the rarified atmosphere above timberline.

The tracks became increasingly difficult to follow, and the air thinner. His lungs began to work harder and Tony stumbled, affected as well by the leanness of the oxygen. Horne's vision blurred and the faint tracks swam away, out of focus, like skittering crayfish beneath the murky waters of a stream. He held Tony to a walk, and rested him every fifteen minutes as they traversed the open tundra above the treeline, bent under the wind's lash like a single sculpture, pulled by gravity, sliding slow across a tilted surface.

Two hours later, somehow, Horne reached the saddle between a jagged line of granite peaks, and headed for the cradle that marked the pass. He no longer worried about tracking Red Hawk. This was the way he would come unless he planned to winter in the high country, an almost certainly fatal mistake. No, Horne reasoned, the Arapaho would head for lower ground, for the camp he and his braves left when they went on the warpath. Horne had known some of their favorite haunts, but in the years since, the encroachment of civilization had probably driven them to seek other encampments.

The storm held back, gathering force in its winds and building clouds that would rupture when conditions were right. Horne crossed the desolate cradle late in the afternoon, picked up the tracks again. The Arapaho had ridden through single–file the night before, or early that morning. One set of tracks, superimposed upon the others, was fresher, less than two hours old. Seven Stars, he figured, and he was pushing his pony.

The tracks veered off, and Horne followed them, curious. At the base of a craggy outcropping, he found Red Hawk's night camp, and here, the tracks were all fresh. Excited, Horne dismounted and studied each depression carefully. Here, he reasoned, Red Hawk had waited for his scouts. And here, Seven Stars had told him that Gray Wolf was on his trail.

Horne found a flat rock that would hold water in its ancient dimple, and poured water from his canteen into the natural bowl for Tony. He fed the horse a handful of grain out of his hat, let him blow and rest as the wind swept across the flat like an invisible scythe, blowing Horne's hair straight back from his face and riffling Tony's mane and forelock.

The man and horse looked as if they were traveling at high speed, even though they were standing still.

Horne smiled, his lips flattened against his face from the wind, and mounted Tony. He had gained some ground, after all. The tracks leading away from the camp were now little more than an hour old. He could see for a long way as he rode across the flat, urging Tony to canter every hundred yards or so.

The first snow flurries blew down on Horne as he started down out of the pass. He kept Tony to a brisk walk, knowing he could push him no harder than that at this altitude. Something ahead caught his eye. The ground here was churned by pony hooves, the fresh dirt giving off scent. Warily, Horne approached the object, wondering if Red Hawk had abandoned the white women after all.

The dark shape moved, shimmered in the gray light of afternoon. The snowflakes thickened as Horne rode toward timberline some eight hundred yards below him where something of man, not of the wilderness, loomed larger and more puzzling as he closed the distance.

The smell told him what the object was that had caught his attention. Tony balked, fought the reins. Horne tapped the horse's flanks, brought him in line. "Steady boy," he said, drawing close enough to see the low stone scaffold, the rippling fur of the buffalo coat, the flapping eagle feathers. Wood Jumper was laid out on fresh–cut spruce boughs placed atop cross–laced limbs. His bow and tomahawk rested alongside his body. His waxen face, the eyes sealed shut in *rigor mortis,* wore an expression of a man sleeping. Snowflakes began to cling to the coat and leggings, lodge in the brows and eyelashes.

Tony stamped the ground, shook his head. The scaffold moved slightly in the wind, its limbs scratching against the stone cairns. Horne had seen enough. The burial place brought back a sudden, unbidden memory. He rode into the timber, found the place where the Arapahos had cut the spruce limbs. One side of the large spruce was stripped, resembled the destruction left by the rub of a bull elk in the rut.

Horne's stomach wrenched with a sudden spasm when he saw the message Red Hawk had left for him. Hanging on the mutilated stubs of the spruce were women's undergarments, slashed to ribbons, pieces of brightly colored cloth that were once parts of dresses. This, then, was Red Hawk's answer: the white women belonged to him.

Horne winced, took a deep, grief–healing breath as the memory of another time rose up in his mind.

It happened during the trading season on the Platte. The Mexicans had brought the whiskey, which they mixed with sugar to make it taste good to the Cheyenne and Arapaho. Horne had been off alone, hunting, rode back to find a drunken camp. His friends had traded off everything they owned for the whiskey. Sleeping Water was gone, taken away by Red Hawk against her will. Found–in–Grass had told him that.

"Red Hawk drank from the burning cup," said Horne's father–in–law. "He became crazy. He went to your lodge and closed the flap. We heard Sleeping Water screaming and then it was quiet. We called to Red Hawk, but he would not come out. He did not let Sleeping Water come out. We heard her weeping. We begged Red Hawk to let her go. We left presents in front of the lodge. He would not come out. He was very drunk."

"Where did he take Sleeping Water?" Horne asked.

"We do not know. He brought her out of your lodge. He drank more firewater. He was mean to everyone. We were all afraid of him. He stabbed Porcupine and he beat Lazy Bear. He rode away and took Sleeping Water with him. He said he was going to trade for more whiskey. We are sorry, Gray Wolf. Our hearts are on the ground that this thing happened."

Horne did not wait for Red Hawk to come back. He rode across the river to the place where the Mexican traders were selling whiskey. He rode past their tents and he asked them if they had seen Red Hawk and Sleeping Water. The Mexicans laughed and said obscene things. They were all drunk and making fun of those drunken Indians who could not stand on their feet and those who could only wobble when they walked.

Finally, Horne found a man who would answer his questions. He was an old man who took care of the horses for the Mexicans. He told Horne that an Indian and a woman had ridden off with some white men. They had all covered the woman, he said, and they were all very drunk. He told Horne where they had gone, north, to do more bad things with the woman.

The men had left a trail a blind man could follow. Horne loaded both of his Spanish pistols, his Hawken, and carried belt and boot knives. He found the men in a cave carved out of the earth by the Platte before it had changed course. There were three of them. Red Hawk was not there. Sleeping Water lay inside the cave, naked, her legs covered with blood.

"Give me the woman," said Horne.

"Go to hell," said a surly man, his tongue thick with drink.

Horne shot him between the eyes with one of the single–shot flintlock pistols. The other two reached for their rifles and Horne shot them both, one with the second pistol, the other with his Hawken from five feet away.

Horne found Sleeping Water's elkskin dress. It was ripped apart. Her face was battered almost beyond recognition. Her eyes were puffed shut, her lips swollen and cracked, the cracks filled with caked blood. She was smeared with blood between her legs and one of her legs was broken. She made no sound as he dressed her. Her breathing was very shallow.

He carried his wife back to camp. She died when he laid

her on the buffalo robe inside his lodge. She never regained consciousness.

Buffalo Woman and some others came to the lodge. They dressed Sleeping Water in a soft doeskin dress, and washed her hair, smoothed out her face, painted it with vermillion to hide the bruises. Horne built a scaffold for Sleeping Water up in the hills, away from prying eyes. He rigged a travois for his horse, gave away all his ponies.

"Take down this lodge," he told Found–in–Grass and the others. "Divide our property among yourselves. I will go away. I will never return. My heart is on the ground for my wife. If I see Red Hawk again I will kill him."

"Red Hawk has already been banished from this tribe," said Found–in–Grass. "He will not come back here."

"I go away to the mountains with my sorrow," said Horne.

He stayed with her that night and wept at her scaffold the next morning when the air was sweet with the scent of prairie flowers. He said goodbye to Sleeping Water and left her there, with the wind blowing her hawk's–feather fan, the fringes on her doeskin dress.

After a time, he rode back down to the Arapaho camp, but the people had gone. He found Sleeping Water's torn elkskin dress that had been left behind because it was bad medicine. The dried blood looked like rust. Someone had cut it up into tatters.

And Horne had wept for Sleeping Water one last time.

CHAPTER 11

THE wind died when the sun set. The snows began to fall in thick steady flakes, wet, clinging. Gradually, the temperature dropped. Soon, the snow covered the tracks Horne was following, buried them under a blanket of ermine. The darkness closed in, wiped away all landmarks. There was danger now for the tracker. He was close, very close, and if he stumbled onto Red Hawk's band in the dark, this likely would be his last trail.

Horne dug one of his 'hawks from his saddlebags. This was a Missouri war hatchet, modeled after the Osage ax he'd traded pelts for in Sante Fe, more than a dozen years before. He chopped blazes on two tall pines that stood close together, then rode westerly, looking for shelter. He blazed every thirty yards, whacking notches three inches high, two inches wide in the pine trunks. The exertion made him sweat, and by the time he had found the big deadfall that was to be his shelter until the storm passed, Horne was drenched underneath his clothing.

He stripped Tony of saddle, bedroll and saddlebags, hobbled him, slipped on a hemp halter with a ten–foot lead rope. He tied the horse on the lee side of a brawny spruce, began to gather firewood. He cut his shavings under the shelter of the deadfall after clearing a spot of snow and pine needles. He stacked squaw–wood on the shavings, struck flint and steel to spark the fine wood. The spark nestled in the shavings and he blew it to flame. The squaw–wood caught and Horne had light to lay out his bedroll, store his saddle and gear. He grained Tony, and for the next hour he gathered firewood. The snow fell steady, but the wind stayed down. Flakes hissed as they struck flames, turned to wispy steam. Horne moved the fire twice to thaw the ground for his blankets. He ate dried jerky, nibbled on hardtack, listened to the tink of snow on his hatbrim, scratched his skin in places as his sweat dried.

He did not look into the fire, but into the dark, and he watched Tony. The horse would tell him if a brave tried to slip up on him. But there was only the silence of the snow–flocked trees around him and the faint throb of his heart as he listened.

A man could die here, he thought. *And no one would know the difference.*

Bridger had said much the same thing, that time Horne wintered with him up on the Blackfoot River in '35 and '36. Cap'n Jim had married Cora, the daughter of that Flathead chief, Insala, that year after rendezvous, and he was feeling fit after Doc Whitman carved that iron arrow out of Bridger's back, all three inches of it. "The doc said it had growed in," Bridger told them, and Horne remembered how Jim had laughed, making no never–mind about it. The game ran out that winter and for a time they were eating dug–up roots and drinking mule blood to get by. Oh, it was a hell of a time, those days, Horne admitted, and he missed some of the men he had known back then, Meek and Kit Carson, and Lucien Fontanelle, Drips, young Josiah Paddock, Old Scratch and his mule, Hannah. Jess Coons, Lem Pickard, Bridger, too, who used to ask Horne to read *Hiawatha* to him, and that Shakespeare book he'd traded a yoke of oxen for on the immigrant trail. Where were they now, he wondered. Where were they now? Dead and gone, some of them, and likely he would have been among 'em if he hadn't killed his best friend.

He hadn't thought of Malcolm in a long time. It was hard to get that face straight in his mind. It had blurred over the years, was something he had pushed down in his mind so much it hardly ever came up again. Rob Malcolm, a kid then, like himself, gangly as a rope, puny, crazy from the siph, coughing from lung disease, blood always on his buckskin sleeves from wiping his mouth after a spell. The kid had hair like rusted wire, and a pair of eyes that looked like charcoal chunks. He had a hairlip that made him talk funny, and some winters you could count his rib bones he was so thin.

Everybody liked Malcolm, and maybe that's why Horne took up with him. *Why in hell didn't he just die of consumption?* Horne had asked himself that question a thousand times since that day he had killed Rob up on the Green and run off like a whipped cur so he wouldn't have to explain what couldn't be explained.

Cap'n Stewart made a pet out of Malcolm at rendezvous. Maybe because they were both Scots, or maybe just because that primping Stewart wanted a bootlick to fetch him his bagpipes and fill his cup with whiskey when he sat at the campfires and told his big dreams of empire to any who would listen.

But Malcolm *was* crazy. He proved that, the day Horne had to kill him.

It snowed all night and all the next day. The cold deepened by morning and Horne had to work hard to bring in firewood. He drank coffee and ate *pemmican* to keep his energy up. He rubbed the frozen snow off Tony's back with the saddle blanket, snubbed him close to the fire during the day. The woods were quiet and the snow kept falling.

The high hard winds blew in the following day after the snow stopped and Horne chopped wood all day, chipping off chunks from the deadfall, fighting off the deadly chill that made his blood run slow, scrambled his thinking and probed toward his center, sucking the heat from him with every gelid gust.

Horne fought off the drowsiness, forced himself to hack, hack, hack the wood to feed the voracious fire. He dared not venture far from the flames, for the wind howled and whipped through the trees, flinging snow and cracking branches until Horne wanted to shout for it to stop and give him peace.

The fire burned low, and to keep from falling asleep Horne got up, started jumping up and down, stamping his feet to sting the blood to movement again. He slapped his arms against his sides, tucked his hands under his armpits. The deadfallen tree, so frozen by the chilling winds, dulled his hatchet, but he managed to knock a few chips out to keep the coals going. There was no relief from the cutting wind. He hung one of his blankets up over the dead tree, but the wind blew it down. Horne cursed, but the wind snatched his words away and left only their ghosts hanging in the mist of his breath, until that too, was gone, leaving him depressed.

One mistake in bad weather like this could kill a man. Horne knew that. The hatchet could slip from his fingers, cut off a hand or an arm, puncture an artery. He could fall asleep and never wake up. He was dehydrated, confused. His mind served up disconnected images, rambling words that didn't make sense and were never spoken. He found his canteen, pulled the wooden stob out. The water was frozen. He placed the wooden vessel near the fire, dug a pan out of his saddlebags, filled it with snow. He shook now, as the cold went deeper toward his core and his teeth rattled uncontrollably. He put the pan atop the dying coals. The wind made them burn fast, turned them into miniature blast furnaces that gave off little heat.

The drifts around him were deep, and he'd burned every twig of squaw–wood within a thirty or forty–yard circumference of his camp. He hallucinated warm hearths, glowing lanterns, blazing campfires. The pot hissed and snapped as the heat warmed the metal, melted the snow. Horne picked up the hatchet and floundered to the base of the deadfall. He scrabbled through the snow, looking for broken off limbs, stumps, anything big that would burn.

He found a chunk of branch buried deep in the snow,

frozen hard to the ground. He wrestled it with lifeless fingers, kicked it, tugged on it. The limb broke free, and he lugged it back to the fire. It was soggy, packed with snow, but he put one end of it on the coals and let the wind fan them. He chipped off a few more slivers of wood from the big tree and tossed them on the coals. He was in danger of frostbite now, he knew. If the log didn't catch, he would ride the wind over the great divide. The goddamned wind.

Horne fell to the ground, rolled into his blankets by the fire, and closed his eyes. He curled up into a ball, drew his knees up to his chest, and shivered, so cold he didn't care whether he lived or died.

The wind gradually died down and the dead log caught fire. The snow water boiled and spewed out steam. The smoke blew into Horne's face. He awoke, choking, gagging on the fumes. The fire blazed warm, licked at his wooden canteen. Horne squatted and picked up the canteen with hands so useless they might have been made of wood. The water inside had thawed, and he drank greedily.

The pain seeped into his fingers and toes as the warmth of the fire penetrated the chilled flesh. He wept from the agony, but his teeth stopped chattering and he knew he would survive. He chopped the log up into manageable lengths and built the fire up to a roaring blaze. He brought Tony in close. The horse shied at the flames, but Horne led him around the fire, in circles, and saw his hide turn sleek as the frozen snow turned liquid.

Later in the afternoon, Tony whickered softly, and Horne saw the elk. They moved through the trees like ghosts, their rumps muddy tawn in the feeble light, their thick brown coats flocked with patches of snow. The elk herd, more than a hundred animals, passed within a hundred yards of Horne's camp, migrating to the lowlands.

He saddled Tony, packed his gear and loaded it on the horse. He warmed the lock on his Hawken, the brace of pistols he carried in his saddlebags, checked the actions.

Satisfied, he mounted up and followed the elk herd down the mountain. He would not need blazed trees to find his way.

In the bleak, cold days following the snowstorm, Horne knew he had lost all chances to pick up the trail of Red Hawk and his band. In his heart, he found the reason why he knew he must follow, even if the journey should lead him straight into hell. He no longer felt hatred for Red Hawk. That had burned out of him a long time ago. Now, he realized that he should have avenged Sleeping Water's death before this. Now, he thought of Red Hawk as a wolf gone rabid, something to be exterminated. The storm brought more than snow and wind. In its fury, in its deadliness, it brought him a mortal calm, a focus that had eluded him before. Red Hawk was a part of him, had been part of him all these years. But he was a cancer to be cut away.

It took Horne a long time to figure out that Red Hawk had become jealous of him when Horne took Sleeping Water for his wife. But the signs were there. He had just not seen them. The lone hunting trip he had taken that time before Sleeping Water died had been Red Hawk's idea. "Go and find the medicine wolf," Red Hawk had said. "Kill him and eat his heart. You will be strong. You will be an Arapaho forever."

Horne had killed the gray wolf, eaten its heart. It had made him sick and he had vomited. He had never told anyone this, but now he thought of it, and wondered if he had spewed up the wolf's heart because he did not want to be an Arapaho forever. The thought gave him comfort as he sought shelter from the snow and wind.

It took him better than two months, after the storm broke, to reach the prairie. He had long since left the elk herd behind, too grateful to take one for meat, too tired to dress one out if he had. Horne found a few traces of Red Hawk and his band. The first was a gutted bull elk carcass that he found at the edge of a meadow, half–buried in the snow, and the tracks long since obliterated by wind and thaw and freeze. Pony tracks led him to the Laramie River and, though he rode for another month while his grain dwindled and his food supplies petered out, he could not find more tracks.

Somewhere between the mountains and the north fork of the Platte, Red Hawk had disappeared. Either he had gone east to the open prairie, or he had doubled back, headed west to the lower North Platte and might even be heading for Bridger's Pass.

Christmas came and went, a new year too, and Horne met traders and hunters who sold him supplies. But none had seen the Arapaho band he sought, none had heard of white women in Indian camps. Seven Stars was right, he thought. Red Hawk's tracks had disappeared like smoke. Horne criss–crossed the plains, trying to pick up the trail, and the months of '53 wore on through spring and summer until Horne found that he had doubled back to the place where he had come down out of the mountains. Again, his supplies ran short and he hadn't seen a white man or Indian since late June.

Horne followed the Laramie north, to the old fort that was called Fort William when he was a boy. It had been named after Bill Sublette, but he'd heard the army had taken it over and named it Fort Laramie. That would have been in '49, right after the Mexican War ended, almost four years ago.

He hunted small game, surprised that summer had not yet seared the plains. The mountains were green and only the high peaks carried mantles of snow. Tony grazed on decent grass, and for a time, Horne did not think of the white girls and what Red Hawk might be doing with them.

CHAPTER 12

LESS than ten miles below the fort, Horne saw them coming. Six or eight horsemen, charged in his direction. Then, he heard the high–pitched cries that sounded like the forlorn calls of black crow. He knew they were Indians by the way they rode their ponies. A thin spool of dust rose over the prairie behind them, grew larger as they approached at full speed.

"Sioux," he said, and clapped Tony's flanks with the heels of his moccasins. The Indians charged along the east bank of the Laramie, then fanned out. There were eight of them, after all. Horne headed for the Platte at full gallop. He heard a shot, turned and saw a puff of smoke. A ball whistled overhead and he kicked Tony again.

He had some advantage. The Indians had been running their ponies longer. If he could reach the Platte River, he might cross it and hold them off. Tony laid his ears back and braced the wind in his teeth. Horne flattened out on the side of his saddle as another shot boomed behind him. The ball fried the air a foot from his ear and the war cries shifted to a higher pitch, turned shrill.

Where in hell are the soldiers? he thought.

He heard the familiar hiss of an arrow shaft as it whiffled by him, saw it arc into the grass and disappear in front of him. A chorus of yelps made the hackles on Horne's neck rise. He turned Tony to the left, reined him to the right, in a zig–zag pattern. He could feel the animal straining under him and knew he could not keep up the pace for long. Ahead, he saw the banks of the North Platte, and, on the other side, a line of wagons and people staring at him.

"Come on, Tony," he said. "Get to the river, boy."

Horse and rider sailed over the bank, galloped into the stream. On the other side, he saw men pointing their rifles at the Sioux. Tony floundered through the shallows, splashing the water high. The current was not strong and they hit no deep water. The Sioux cries grew weaker as they slowed their horses and by the time Horne reached the opposite bank, they were no longer hawking at him like angry crows.

Tony lurched up the bank, onto the flat. Horne turned around, saw the Sioux pull their horses to a halt some two hundred yards away. Then, he looked at the men standing in a line, holding rifles, but none of them taking aim.

"Why in hell don't you shoot?" asked Horne.

"If they attack us, we will discharge our weapons," said a tall, angular man, wearing a flat–brimmed hat and a dark suit. He had a long pointed beard and held a Bible in his hand.

"They're Sioux," said Horne, "and they tried to lift my hair."

"Are you injured?" said the man.

"Just my pride," said Horne.

He turned, slid his rump over the edge of the saddle, felt the tension drain from him. The Sioux brandished their weapons, shook them. He heard them shout some obscenities. A couple of them stood up on their ponies' backs and lifted their breechclouts. The ultimate insult. Then they turned their ponies and rode off as if they had only been out on a lark, chasing rabbits.

"Be thankful to the Lord for sparing you," said the man.

"Who you be?" asked Horne.

"We're Saints," said the man.

"Mormons, eh."

"On our way to the Salt Lake."

"Where are the soldiers? Has the fort been taken?"

"No. We sent one of our brethren up yesterday. He returned this morning. There has been a terrible tragedy here. Come. See for yourself."

The other Mormons walked back to their wagons, but Horne noticed that some of them stood guard atop the seats, rifles at the ready. He had little doubt that they would shoot to defend themselves. He heard the men talking and then he heard the voices of women and children as they came out from their hiding places in the wagons.

Horne dismounted. A young man ran up, took the reins of his horse without speaking. The lean man walked to the other side of the emigrant road and Horne caught the smell. He knew what it was before he even saw the shallow graves. He saw several pairs of soldiers' gloves lying in the grass. Some of the men's heads were not even covered with dirt, but their bodies had been picked over by buzzards and coyotes. Swatches of torn uniforms lay in shreds among the graves. Broken arrows littered the earth. Some were smeared with dried blood, clear to the feathered vanes. There was a man's head, severed from his body, lying on the bank of a grave with the teeth grinning hideously, and the flesh torn off of his face.

"What happened here?" Horne asked quietly.

"A massacre. I'm Brother Empey, and we have been hearing about it for half a month. Your name, Sir?"

"Horne."

"Mister Horne, there are twenty–nine soldiers buried here with their officer, a lieutenant named Grattan. For the past several days, we have been armed and conducting defense drills among our men. Brother Charles Brererton is wagon master and I have appointed Brother Campbell as president of this company. Several nights ago, just below here, we were visited by Sioux Indians who came into our camp."

"What about Fort Laramie? Any soldiers left there?"

"Come, we'll speak to Brother Cook, our first councillor. He returned from the fort a few moments ago."

Horne sucked in a deep breath. He turned away from the graves, followed Empey to the head of the wagon train. He noticed that both sides of the road were well guarded by men with rifles.

In the shade of the lead wagon, a group of men squatted around one who was washing the grime from his face. At their approach, the men nodded and walked away, leaving only the one whose shirt was stained with sweat.

"Brother Cook, this is Mister Horne. He would like to know what you saw at Fort Laramie."

Horne shook hands with Cook, sized him up. He was a small, intent man, with the empty face of an ascetic, dark–browed, wearing a full beard. His black coat hung over a wagon wheel. It matched his trousers. His shirt was gray muslin, wrinkled and damp.

"There are only forty–two soldiers in the fort," said Cook. He continued to swab his neck, dabbed behind his ears with the washcloth. "They seem to have only scanty provisions. They would not sell us flour for under twenty dollars the hundred. There's a post office and a sutler's store there. They're waiting for a higher officer to come in and tell them what to do. There were, until a few days ago, several thousand Indians camped around the fort."

"What stirred the Injuns up?" asked Horne.

Cook stood up, wrung out the washcloth. He looked up at Horne, his brown eyes dull with worry.

"On August seventeenth, three, four weeks ago, we met a company of thirty–three wagons returning to the states from Fort Laramie. They had taken provisions there for the government. Everything was all right then, but they told us there was some trouble with the Indians over a cow. One of the Saints that had passed through said a Sioux had killed it. Six days later, we encountered ten more wagons, and they said some soldiers had gone into the Indian camp and hadn't come back."

"That's right," said Empey. "We were very apprehensive.

The wagoneers told us to hold up, but we are bound for the holy land."

"On the twenty–seventh," said Cook, "we met some mountaineers. They were carrying dispatches from the fort telling about Lieutenant Grattan's massacre. Two nights ago, we met some Sioux Indians. They had firearms and acted very hostile. Brother Brererton stopped the train. Then a chief and six braves came into camp."

"We treated them kindly," said Empey. "Having received plenty to eat and drink, they made signs that they wished to go to sleep. Brother Campbell gave his tent to them."

"Was that the end of it?" asked Horne.

"On first September," said Cook, "the very next day, we encountered more hostiles. We did not move far until we met the Indians on every side of us. They were all on horseback and well armed. They blockaded the road in front of us, but every man in camp carried his rifle loaded on his shoulder and we drove right through them. Brother Campbell exchanged hands with them after which he made a call on every wagon to give the savages a portion of sugar. The Indians kept following us until dinner time and stated that they were going to war with another nation."

"We determine that to mean our government," said Empey.

Horne nodded in agreement. He did not like the sound of it. Any of it.

"Nigh ten days ago," said Cook, "we met a company of men, mules and ox teams going to the states. We also met the Indian agent who advised us to be on the lookout as the Indians had left Fort Laramie and had gone, no one knows where. He himself was obliged to make his escape from them."

"You goin' on?" asked Horne.

"Yes, but we'll not stop by the fort," said Empey. "There's a station on the Platte above it where we'll bide a day. Our women and children are shocked and frightened."

"I'm obliged for the news," said Horne. He shook hands with Empey and Cook.

"Where are you bound?" asked Cook.

"I'll stop at Bordeau's if he's still tradin', maybe go to the fort."

"You are hunting, Sir?" asked Empey.

"I am. Arapaho."

"Eh, what's that?"

"Injun, name of Red Hawk. He's got him three white girls."

"What will you do if you catch him?" asked Cook.

"I'll kill him," said Horne, and walked away to get his horse.

Three hundred yards away stood Bordeau's trading post. Men with rifles stood atop it, on guard. As he rode away from the wagon train, Horne saw the signs that there had been a recent Indian camp there. He could smell it and the ground was laced with pony and travois tracks, flattened by the soles of many moccasins. The Indians would consider this a great victory, he knew. They were already bragging about going to war. If the Sioux were in it, so were the Cheyenne, and the Arapaho.

He realized, with a feeling that he was sinking into a quagmire, that if he did not find Red Hawk soon, the Arapaho would go on the warpath with his people and Horne might never get the white girls back.

A man at Bordeau's hailed him.

"Who air ye, stranger?" Horne recognized the voice.

"I was mothered by a she–painter, fathered by the meanest he–bear in the mountains," Horne replied. "And I eat all but free trappers for breakfast."

"Horne? Be that you, Jackson Horne?"

"Jess Coons, you better put that fusil away 'fore you shoot yourself in the foot."

The man on the platform behind the barricade jumped up and down, hollered with glee.

"Damn, son, I thought ye was plumb dead and here ye air, bright as a chunk of Mexican silver, still wearin' yore dadgummed hair."

Horne frowned, rode up to the post. The gate opened and he trotted Tony inside the enclosure. Jess Coons jumped down from the platform, approached him, grinning, in his wobbly, bow–legged gait. He appeared genuinely glad to see Horne.

But Jess Coons was the last man on earth Horne wanted to see.

CHAPTER 13

JESS COONS had lost some teeth since Horne had last seen him. Some weight, too, and he'd grown a heap more lines in his grizzled face, maybe shrunk up some. His blue eyes had that same crackle to them though, and he looked at home in his Cree hunting coat and cotton trapper's shirt. Both garments were begrimed with fat juices and tobacco. His fringed buckskin trousers drooped over his hard–sole moccasins. He wore a wide leather belt and a Green River knife sheath, both studded with brass tacks. His possibles pouch hung at his side. He still carried the heavy plains rifle he'd lugged when he was a free trapper.

"Waugh, Horne, you old sumbitch," yelled Coons, "you know damned well I'm the meanest chile ever to set foot on a mountain. I can ride a thunderstorm, swim 'crost lava, outshoot and outfight any man, bear or wolf. I am some."

Men, some more Indian than white, rushed out to greet the visitor, surrounded him.

"Howdy, old salt," said John Paul Sanderson, separating himself from the other mountain men. "See you kept yore curly hair."

Sanderson's eyes were rheumy from drink, his complexion sallow, yellowish. He had aged more than Coons. He wore a shirt of decorated elkhide, north plains leggings. His moccasins were soft soled. A pipe bag hung from his belt, beaded in Cheyenne design. He carried his rifle in a fringed buckskin sheath, his possibles in a fringed buffalo–hide bag. Both he and Coons wore low crown felt hats with wide brims.

Horne swung out of the saddle. Coons embraced him,

then Sanderson. Sanderson reeked of whiskey fumes. Other men slapped Horne on the back. One of them took his horse. He found himself being jostled along to the main house, flanked by Coons and Sanderson.

"What brings you out from under the rocks?" asked Sanderson. "You aim to fight Injuns?"

"I'm lookin' hard for one," said Horne.

"We got us some Mex brandy what'll loosen yore tongue, Horne," said Coons. "John Paul, you shet yore mouth 'til we set this feller down for some fat chewin'."

"Hell," groused Sanderson, "I thought the chile was done gone over the mountain."

They entered a storehouse which was almost empty of trade goods. Instead, it held traps and tools belonging to the mountain men, powder, ball, rifles, buffalo robes, blankets. There was a table, some chairs, a few sacks of sugar and grain. The floor was littered with powder and cracked corn. The adobe walls were cracked and showed the marks where sacks had been stacked. Cobwebs dangled from the high corners. A wooden case of brandy lay opened near the table. Coons lifted a bottle from the packing straw, bit out the cork. He took a swig, passed the bottle to Horne. Horne drank, felt the fire burn down his throat, hit his stomach like acid. He choked, gave the bottle to Sanderson.

" 'Bout the onliest thing them redskins didn't get," said Coons. "They cleaned out Bordeau, put the fear in him. You heerd about it, Horne?"

"Some. I run into the Mormons down the road."

"I 'spec that was you a–runnin' from them Brulés. Wal, thet's the last of them. The Sioux pulled out from the fort awhile ago. Still a bunch of Cheyenne and 'Rappyhoe camped out. They got them soljer boys plumb frighted."

"What the hell happened here?" asked Horne.

"Me'n John Paul here, we come in after'n it happened. We run into some Minniconjou runners full o' war talk and they tole us old Bear That Scatters got kilt, and then the Brulés and the Minniconjou plumb went crazy and killed half the soljers in the fort."

"Thet be so," said Sanderson.

"We come on in and Bordeau said the Injuns cleaned him out after the fight, took most of his tradin' stock. Lucky them redskins didn't kill him, I reckon."

"It all started over a damned Mormon cow," said Sanderson. "Coulda all been handled peaceable but Grattan took cannon into camp and the Brulé got their dander up. Bordeau tole us the lieutenant took Lucien Auguste to interpret."

"That halfbreed chile was drunk," said Coons. "He aggravated them Sioux, pure and plain."

Horne listened as the bottle was passed and the two men told him how Bordeau had barricaded his doors to defend himself. The Indians, following the fight, rode up and wanted to burn his station to the ground, but other Indians spoke up for him. Some of the traders had Indian wives and they pleaded for him, too. The Indians stripped him of goods, however, and took a lot of whiskey with them. "Then the Sioux broke into the American Fur warehouses up by the fort and just took their annuities in advance. They went on a spree up the Platte and stole from the government farm. They turned plumb mean, Horne, and it ain't gonna stop here. The soljers are waitin' for a big chief to come in and take after the Sioux."

"The soljers is building a blockhouse," added Sanderson. "We got us a war here, son."

"You stayin' to git in it, Jackson?" asked Coons, pointblank, his blue eyes glittering like sunstruck turquoise.

"I got other fish to fry, Jess."

"Eh? Chile, this whole prairie's gonna run blood. You got yer rifle and a purty good horse. Army's gonna need scouts. Ye can fill yore belly, git reg'lar pay and tear off some hair."

"Maybe he's gonna run like he did before," said Sanderson belligerently.

"John Paul, they ain't no need to bring up that bizness," said Coons.

"Well, he damned shore snuck off after'n he kilt young Rob Malcolm. Never tole his friends a damned word."

Horne fixed Sanderson with a murderous look. Coons cleared his throat, took another drink of brandy. Sanderson shrugged and looked away. It was quiet in the room for several moments.

"I'm lookin' for a buck named Red Hawk," said Horne evenly, waving the proffered bottle away. "He's took him three white girls. Thought he might have come this way."

" 'Rappyhoe," said Coons. "Know some of him all right. Bad one. White gals, ye say? Injun agent come in with fifteen thousand pounds of goods, made a palaver with the Cheyenne. The Injuns tole him they wanted no more whites on the Platte road. Tole him to bring them four thousand dollars next year and one thousand white squaws they could have for wives. 'Pears to me these redskins got 'em a taste for white meat."

"Red Hawk knows I'm on his track," said Horne.

"You might see Newcastle. He's got him a tradin' post down the Platte, 'bout eighteen mile."

"Newcastle?"

"Yep. Hardy Newcastle. He trades with the 'Rappyhoe. In pertic'alar, that buck Red Hawk. Lem Pickard's due in tonight from the fort. He can take you on down, it bein' important, mebbe. One of them gals b'long to ye, Horne?"

"No," he replied. "You say Lemuel's here?"

"Been doin' the interpretin' with the Cheyenne. He don't hold nothin' against you, Horne. None of us does. You done the right thing, killin' Malcolm. Oh, some was all fer chasin' after yer, right off, but after we tole them what happened, they cooled down. Everybody thought he was a nice lad and here he was a cold–blooded killer. Long before he come to rendezvous with them Blackfeet gals. Yep, Lem he wrote a letter back to Rob's folks in Kaintuck' and he got back a letter from the law a–sayin' they was dead and Rob was the one what kilt 'em. Cut up his ma and pa and little sister and then run to the mountains. Yessir, that sumbitch was a killer, all right. Imagine, killin' your own kin up close like that."

Horne sat back in his chair, stunned. Sanderson took the bottle, drank from it, began to nod his head. Coons squinted, wrinkling the skin around his eyes as he studied Horne intently.

"A long time ago, Jack," said Jess. "A long time ago and a lot of rivers done been crost."

"We knew the sumbitch had them Blackfeet gals," said Sanderson. "He kilt one of 'em."

"Huh?" asked Horne. "No, no he didn't."

"Yep," said John Paul. "You couldna done nothin' 'bout thet. We found her bloody body all hacked up, floatin' down the Green. Rob done it all right. He done caught him three Blackfeet gals, raped and kilt one before anyone knew."

"There were only two," said Horne softly. "I saw only two."

He remembered the look in Malcolm's eyes.

"Horne, come looky what I got," he said. "God, I got me some nice ones. Real bitches."

"What in hell you jawin' about, Rob?"

"You foller me. Oh, sweet Judas Priest, Jackson you got to see this."

Horne followed Malcolm way up Horse Creek, past the tents and stock, past the carousing men, into thick brush. Rob had made a lean–to, and there were two Blackfeet girls lying on buffalo robes, bound and gagged. Rob had made a kind of shrine out of it, decorated it with feathers tied to leather thongs, empty bottles. It was a strange and sickening place, even before Horne knew what Malcolm was up to.

"I caught 'em, Jack. Caught 'em myself. Lordy, look at 'em. Ripe."

"Those are Blackfeet, Rob. Better turn 'em loose or take 'em back."

That's when Rob had pulled his dirk. His eyes gleamed with madness. Saliva spilled out of the corners of his mouth, drooled down his chin. He started for the girls, but Horne grabbed his arm.

"Don't joke, Rob," he said.

Malcolm wrenched away, knocked Horne down. His sudden strength was startling. He made an odd growling sound in his throat. Horne jumped up, pulled the Spanish pistol from his belt. The lock was a miguelet pattern. It was fitted with a belt hook, had brass sideplates, an ornamented French–style tanged butt–cap. He had never drawn it on a man before.

"I'm going to cut their innards out," slobbered Malcolm.

"Rob, if you touch either of those girls, I'm going to blow your idiot brains out."

Malcolm cocked his arm, raised the knife above his head, poised to plunge the blade into one of the girls' breast. Horne cocked his pistol, but Malcolm, oblivious to all else, brought his arm down. Horne fired. The ball struck Malcolm in the right temple. The .60 caliber ball tore through Rob's skull, blew out his brains in a pink spray of blood. The explosion was deafening to Horne's ears. It seemed to him that everyone in the world must have heard it.

Malcolm pitched forward, the knife falling from his dead fingers. Horne stepped through the cloud of smoke. He rammed the pistol back on his belt, drew his knife. He cut the girls free, made sign with his hands. They were both very beautiful and they trembled with fear. "Run," he said in English. "Run like hell."

He looked at Malcolm and the bile rose up in his throat.

He stepped outside the lean–to and vomited. He realized he had not been talking to the Blackfeet girls, but to himself. He raced back to his camp, packed up his gear and caught up his horse.

"I ran like hell," Horne said aloud, as he jolted out of his reverie.

"Eh, what's thet?" asked Sanderson.

"I was thinkin' about that day," said Horne. "I figured William Drummond Stewart would have my scalp for killin' Malcolm."

"Haw!" cried Coons. "They was a halfbreed kid saw ever'thing that happened up there on the Horse. He took off, too, but he got drunk that night and tole us what you done. Boy, you was a hero and we drank to you. This kid got scared the next day and he lit a shuck. We found the other Blackfeet girl and she was carved up hideous."

"I didn't see anyone there," said Horne.

"He seen Malcolm cotch them gals, and he seed him kill that one. He saw you go up there to thet lean–to with Rob and spied on you. Like a mouse he was, and plumb curious."

"Did the kid have a name?" asked Horne.

"Yair," said Sanderson. "He was called Jules."

"That's right!" exclaimed Coons. "His name was Jules Moreaux. Hell of a trapper. With Bridger's bunch, I recollec'."

"Jules Moreaux," said Horne. "Well, I'll be damned."

"You knowed him?"

"Not then," said Horne. "I wonder why he never said anything."

"Hell, that ain't a thing a man talks about ever' day," said Coons.

"No," said Horne. "I think I'll take another swig of that Mexican brandy, Jess."

"Hell, drink all you want. Stay the night."

Horne drank and felt a great weight lift from his shoulders. After all the years of wondering his mind seemed to open, free itself of the tangles that choked it, that gave him the terrible nightmares.

He was glad now he had let those Blackfeet girls go. He was glad he had shot Robert Malcolm and killed him dead.

He thought of the Simmons girls then, and wondered if his life was not coming full circle. It seemed he had ridden this trail before and maybe was fated to follow it all the rest of his days.

CHAPTER 14

LEMUEL PICKARD was one of those men who appear to have been born old. Horne could see no change in the man after a dozen years. He was still scrawny–lean, still half–bald, still half–Indian in his dress, still toothless as a prairie chicken. But the man filled a door and cast a long shadow.

"See you tooken to caplock, Horne," he said. " 'Bout time mebbe so."

"Lem, you don't look no different. Don't talk no different either." Horne unscrewed the cleaning jag from his ramrod, wiped the Hawken down as Pickard entered the room. He wore 'skins, a fustian–cloth shirt, beaver hat that looked as if the moths had gotten to it, hard–sole boot moccasins. His possibles bag hung below his beltline. He wore a big knife and the same old pipe bag. Coons and Sanderson were lying like camp dogs on buffalo robes, tin plates of partially–eaten food nearby on the floor.

"You ain't a mountain man no more?"

"Settler," said Horne. "Raise horses, trap some."

Lemuel leaned his rifle against the wall, sat across the table from Horne. His narrowed dark eyes didn't miss much. "You alluz was able to talk mountain man, but I know you was eddicated, Horne. 'Member you readin' poems and sech to Bridger."

"Man uses what he needs, when he needs it."

"Rightly so. Bridger was here this summer, ast about you, Jack. He was livened up by this Irisher what rode into Laramie. Dandy sportsman. Brung him six wagons, twenty–one carts, twelve yoke of cattle, a hundred and twelve horses, fourteen dogs and forty servants. Called hisself Sir George Gore."

"Haw!" laughed Horne. "What did old Jim think of that?"

"They argied some. 'Bout Shakespeare. Bridger reckin'd he was too highfalutin' for him. He said thet he 'rather calcerlated that that big Dutchman, Mr. Full–stuff, was a lettle too fond of lager beer,' and thought it would have been better for the old man if he had 'stuck to bourbon whiskey straight.' "

"Bridger can call his own tunes," said Horne, setting his Hawken down.

"What brings you upriver, son?"

Horne told him. He asked if it would be worth his while to go down the Platte and look up Hardy Newcastle. Coons began to snore. Sanderson joined in as if the two sleepers had practiced playing nose music. Lem took out his clay pipe, filled it with tobacco, lit it with the candle burning on the table. He blew the smoke out through the fine hairs that sprouted from his nostrils, and out the sides of his mouth.

"You best ride down there now, whilst the sun's down. We got Injuns hell–bent on clearin' the emigrant road. Newcastle trades with Red Hawk, fer sart'in sure. I heered Caleb McGonigle's name spoke a time er two. Hardy's brother Luke did the tradin' fer that Scot."

Horne's eyes closed to slits; his jawline hardened.

"Explains some things, maybe," he said.

"Hardy ain't one to tangle with. If Red Hawk come to the flats, he'd likely get his supplies from that'un."

"Much obliged, Lem," said Horne. "I'd best be goin', then. My saddlebags and canteens are full. I got plenty of powder and caps."

"You be keerful, son. Mebbe you'll live a long life. You done a good thing when you kilt that kid, Malcolm. I alluz thought his brain was set with a leetle too much Kaintucky windage."

"A man can't do much about the length of his life," said

Horne. "But he can damned sure do something about its width and depth."

"Rightly so, Jack. Rightly so."

Horne picked up the Hawken, dug out the measure from his possibles, put the horn peg between his teeth, jerked it out. He poured powder into the measure. From the measure he poured a hundred grains down the barrel. He slapped the stock hard to settle the powder. He patched a ball, rammed it six inches down the barrel with the short starter. He seated ball and patch on the powder with his ramrod. He put his things away, stood up.

Lem blew a plume of smoke at the candle flame. He did not rise.

"Watch yore topknot, Horne," he said.

"I'll do that, Lem."

"Be seein' you bye n' bye, I reckon. You'll do all right. Just follow the burnin' cup, you want Red Hawk. He loves his whiskey and the wimmin."

"One or the other will be the death of him," said Horne as he shouldered his saddle bags and canteens. He stalked from the room.

Lem's laughter followed him out, into the night. The moon was on the wax, a shining sliver of fingernail in the sky. The stars shone bright across the inky sky like distant settlements on a vast prairie.

Horne saddled up Tony, snugged his gear up tight so that nothing rattled. The guard let him out wordlessly, and Horne rode east along the Platte, over the emigrant road that now seemed cursed. Even on the windless night air, he could smell the soldiers' blood.

Horne rode off the trail well past midnight. He hobbled Tony, then slept. When the dawn broke, he was back on the emigrant road. Familiar landmarks began to appear and Horne felt the tension. He rode to the river, looked across. This was the place where Sleeping Water had died. Not far from here was where he had put her body on the scaffold.

Some inner compulsion gnawed at Horne. He looked around him. He could almost see the Arapaho camp shimmering in the morning sun. He could hear the laughter, see the children playing, smell the smoke rising through the smoke–holes of the *tipis*.

He crossed the Platte, rode up into the low hills where he had said goodbye to Sleeping Water. He would not have been able to explain his reasons to anyone. He came to the place, his stomach muscles tightened, his belly quivering underneath.

The morning wind rose up, sweeping down from the mountains. He looked into the distance, saw the green trees, the bright yellow leaves of the aspen flickering golden in the sun. A sadness crept over him, and he forced himself to ride to the place where he had put the scaffold.

There was no trace of Sleeping Water's ever having been there. Time and the weather's way, the buzzards and other critters, had erased all evidence of the burial. It was just as well, Horne thought. It was bad enough just being here on this desolate hill of ghostly memories.

Tony's ears perked, twisted to pick up the sound. Horne eased the Spanish pistol from his belt. He rested his thumb on the hammer, listened.

"Gray Wolf," said a voice speaking in the Arapaho tongue. "You have come."

"My eyes do not see who calls my name," replied Horne in Arapaho.

An old man walked from a copse of alder, his eagle feather bonnet flashing in the sun. His face was wrinkled from many winters, his small eyes sunken into a skeletal face. He wore beaded buckskins, carried only a pipe in his withered hands.

"Son, I am Found–in–Grass. Do you not know my face?"

"Father, I know you."

"Let us smoke the pipe. Let us make talk. Only my shadow falls on this ground."

"I am alone, too." Horne dismounted, ground–tied Tony

to a bush. The old man found a place of shade, sat down. Horne hunkered down beside him, watched as he sprinkled tobacco into his hand, offered it to the four directions before filling his bowl. He struck a flint on a curved piece of steel, lit the long pipe, smoked, and then passed the pipe to Horne.

They smoked the pipe down before Found–in–Grass spoke slowly and with great effort. His breath wheezed through fragile lungs, whistled through his thin nostrils.

"The old woman is dead. Weasel–Bear has gone to the spirit world also. Our people are scattered. We live off the goods the white man brings to the fort. The buffalo are few. I have had no antelope meat in six snows. Some of our people have gone with the Lakota and the Cheyenne to fight the white eyes."

He fell silent. "Why are you here?" asked Horne.

"I came to this place to give up my spirit," Found–in–Grass said. "I will go to sleep soon."

"You knew I would come here?"

"I thought you would come here. I have seen Red Hawk. He was here."

"Here? When?"

"During the last sun. He hunts you, Gray Wolf. He knows you want the white women."

"Where is he?" asked Horne, his voice barely audible.

"He goes to the trading post this sun."

Horne knew he was no more than three or four miles from Newcastle's Station. He could easily beat Red Hawk there, wait for him.

"Why does Red Hawk go to the trading post?"

"He will trade one of the white women for goods. Then he will go to the mountains, to the Medicine Bows, stay in the small hills."

"Why do you tell me all this, old man?"

"Because Red Hawk killed my daughter. He has been banished from our people, but he still makes trouble. He takes the white women and the Arapaho are made guilty when it is not their doing."

"Gray Wolf understands."

"Leave now. By setting sun, Red Hawk will be at the white man's trading post on the other side of the river."

"Goodbye, my father."

"My heart is full, my son. I will leave my bones in this place where my daughter's spirit still haunts the earth."

Horne mounted up, rode down the hill. He looked back, once, but Found–in–Grass was not there. Shadows moved across the deserted hillside as clouds passed over the sun. The alder thicket swayed, but it was only the wind rustling the limbs and leaves.

The emigrant road was deserted. The trading post stood desolate on the empty plain, its grayed logs shining in the sun. Horne heard a dog bark. The hitchrail caught the shadows of the structure. A lizard darted down its length, squirted away as Horne approached. He smelled the reek of corn mash, the acrid scent of charred wood. The sign tacked onto the front of the small stockade read *Newcastle Station.* The door was shut.

Horne jerked the Hawken from its sheath. He tied Tony to the rail, strode to the door. He pounded on it with the butt of his Hawken. The door swung open a crack.

"The post is closed," said a voice. A man peered out at Horne. Horne pushed him away, stepped inside. "Hey, mister, don't you hear good?"

"Unless you're Newcastle, stand aside," said Horne.

"I work for the man."

"You want to keep breathing, get out of my way," said Horne.

The man looked at Horne for a long moment then went outside. Horne dropped the latch into place. He looked around, saw the wagons and mules. There were signs that someone had been loading the wagons. Boxes and cases of goods lay in the beds, on the ground. A calico–spotted dog growled at him, then slunk away. Inside the main building, Horne heard the sounds of bottles clinking.

Hardy Newcastle looked up from the box he was loading with whiskey bottles atop the long bar, saw the doorway fill with the silhouette of the tall man carrying the Hawken, a brace of pistols on his belt.

"How did you get in here, mister? This goddamned post is closed. Haven't you heard? Every damned tribe of Injun you ever heard of is fixin' to burn this prairie to a crisp."

"I heard. You Newcastle?"

"I sure am. Who in hell are you?"

"I'm Horne."

Newcastle paled. His lower lip trembled. One of his hands moved and Horne let his right hand fall to the butt of his pistol.

"Think real hard, Newcastle," said Horne, fixing the man with a daggering look, "and then think twice more."

CHAPTER 15

NEWCASTLE swallowed, held his hands steady. He was a medium-built man, with a rawboned face streaked with red blotches, dark shaggy hair, graying eyebrows, and mutton-chop sideburns.

"Buy you a drink?" he said.

"You don't resemble your brother much," said Horne.

"Luke? He favors our ma."

"He the one told you about Sky Valley?"

"First off, yair, I reckon so. He likes it up there, but he likes the money we got down here."

"Partners?"

"You could say that. He brings me business from here and yon."

"McGonigle used to trade with a Cherry Creek outfit that came up to Fort Collins once a month," Horne pressed. He was putting it together, needed confirmation. He strode toward Newcastle, his hand still resting on his pistol butt. Outside, he heard a mule kick, then the whine of the dog.

Newcastle laughed harshly, poured a drink in an empty shot glass, shoved the glass toward Horne very slowly. He kept his hands above the bar, but Horne didn't trust him.

"Feller name of Smoot. Had an accident. I took over, sold to McGonigle. We make and buy better stuff. Look Horne, what's the point?"

"You seen Red Hawk lately?"

"Nope. Not in about three months, two, maybe. He comes, he goes."

"Red Hawk knew about Sky Valley," said Horne. "He knew there was whiskey there."

"I reckon. Sure."

"He was there. He killed McGonigle, a young boy."

"The hell you say."

"He knew where to go. He took three white girls with him when he left."

"Them gals Luke was always talkin' about? Simmons, was it?"

"Yeah."

"Red Hawk, why he plumb likes women. White women, red, makes no difference."

Horne didn't take the drink. The more he listened to Hardy Newcastle, the more he disliked him. The man made him feel dirty, as if he had just wallowed in carrion.

"Seems to me you and your brother got something to account for."

"Mister, I got two wagons left out there. The rest of my people lit a shuck last night. If you didn't run Elmer off, we got work to do. The Injun agent told us to head for Fort Kearny fast as we could get movin'. Man–Afraid–of–His–Horses come by here day afore yestiddy, said the same thing. We're sittin' on a powder keg here and I don't want to be around when the Sioux, the Cheyenne and the Arapaho all go on the warpath. Drink your drink and clear out."

Horne felt the anger rise in him. He didn't like the feeling.

"Red Hawk's on his way here now, Newcastle."

"Maybe."

"You knew he was coming?"

"I didn't say that, Horne."

"Listen, Newcastle, you're just about an inch away from getting the raw end of my temper. Unless you talk straight, I've got some advice for you."

"What's that?"

"You got any favorite prayers made up, you better say 'em now."

"Iron Knife come in here last night. He said Red Hawk's

got some white women to trade. I told him he'd have to make it quick."

"Was he going to trade all three of them? Or just one?"

"One, two, three . . . hell, I don't know. What difference does it make?"

"You trade with an Injun like that, what do you do with the women?"

"Depends."

"That's no answer, Newcastle." Horne struggled to hold his temper. He still felt like he was wallowing in a pile of wormy, stinking meat.

"It's all the answer you're going to get, Horne," said Newcastle, his eyes flickering.

Horne heard the sound behind him, went into a crouch. Elmer stood in the doorway, a rifle pointed at Horne's back. Out of the corner of his eye, he saw Newcastle reach down behind the bar. It all happened so fast, he wasn't aware of moving his hands. He dropped the Hawken, grabbed for his pistols, jerked them free, thumbs cocking them as he raised the barrels. He shot Elmer just as the hired man squeezed the trigger of his heavy plains rifle. Smoke and flame poured into the room. Elmer staggered back through the doorway, a hole in his shirt at a spot over his heart.

Horne wheeled as Newcastle came up with the double-barreled Greener. Twin hammers clicked back, locked, and Horne fired from six feet away. The ball ripped into Hardy Newcastle's throat, ripping out his windpipe, blowing chunks of his spine in all directions. Hardy was blown back into the shelves of bottles. He opened his mouth, but no sound came out—only a bubble of blood that burst as his eyes went wide one last time before frosting over with the glaze of death.

Newcastle slowly slid down the cabinet and crumpled to the floor. Horne held his breath for several seconds, but the Greener didn't go off. Sweat oiled his forehead, sogged his brows. The dog sniffed at Elmer's corpse, whined.

"Git!" yelled Horne. The dog yipped as if it had been kicked, tucked its tail between its legs and ran away to hide.

It was quiet in the room. Horne stepped to the bar, picked up the jigger of whiskey. He tasted it on the tip of his tongue, spat it out.

He looked down at Hardy Newcastle's contorted face.

"You didn't even make good whiskey," he said.

Horne worked fast. He ran the dog outside the stockade, brought Tony in, hid him in the stables. He left the mules and wagons where they were.

He reloaded his pistols, set them on the bar, facing the door. He took the Greener from Newcastle's dead hands, eased the hammers back down, placed the shotgun on the bar. Then he recocked the weapon. He dragged the bodies of both men to a back storeroom, boarded up all the windows, save the one by the door, made the room dark. He took Elmer's rifle, loaded the .58 caliber with eighty grains of priming powder. A hot load, and it might kick hell out of him, but he wanted it to shoot fast and straight.

He cleared space between the bar and the door, kicked boxes aside. He found a trade musket, packed it with powder and cut up several silver trinkets, stuffed them down the barrel for shot. He cocked that weapon and set it on the bar with the others. Finally, he set the Hawken close at hand, next to one of his pistols.

Then Horne waited. He thought of Sleeping Water, of Found–in–Grass dying in the hills across the river, and Buffalo Woman, dead now, and Weasel–Bear, gone too. He thought of Rob Malcolm and wondered at the twisted brain of a man who could knife his folks to death without blinking an eye, cut up a Blackfoot girl just for the pure enjoyment of it. He wondered, too, about a man like Red Hawk, gone bad from the white man's whiskey. Who did you blame? One man could take a drink and walk away. Another went crazy. What did you do with a dog that goes rabid? You kill it, but you hate the disease, not the dog.

He thought that was the way it was with Red Hawk, with Malcolm. But a man was given his life and he was given choices. Roads to take. Sometimes a man went too far down the wrong road. Red Hawk had done this. He drank from the burning cup and it took away his pride. In his way, he was as sick, as crazy as Malcolm. A hydrophobic dog, no good to itself anymore, nor to anyone else. If you let such an animal go, it would infect other animals.

Horne would take no pleasure in killing Red Hawk, if it came to that. His death would not bring back Sleeping Water, or Caleb McGonigle, or little Angus MacPherson.

During that long afternoon, Horne made himself a promise. If Red Hawk came and Horne lived through it, he would do something he should have done when Sleeping Water died. He would burn this whiskey trading post to the ground.

He heard the drum of pony hooves on the earth. Heard the cackle of Arapaho voices, the laughter as they rode up. He heard the ponies come through the gate, into the enclosure.

"Hardeee!" called Red Hawk. "Eh, white trader, we come!"

Horne picked up the Greener, backed slowly into the shadows. He hunched low behind the bar, looked through the window. His throat tightened when he saw one of the girls astride a pony.

"Hardeee!"

Horne held his breath. His finger curled around the front trigger of the shotgun. He heard the braves talking in Arapaho. Red Hawk told them to look inside.

"He is drunk. He sleeps," said Seven Stars.

One of the braves laughed. Horne heard wood and leather creak as some of the warriors dismounted. They padded through the door, shading their eyes. None carried bows or rifles. Red Hawk did not come in, but sat his pony. Horne saw him through the window. The Indian looked right at him, but Horne knew that he couldn't see through the darkness.

Iron Knife, Crow Caller, Gray Elk, Diving Eagle and Seven Stars entered the room, looked around, squinting to adjust their eyes to the absence of light. They looked at the whiskey bottles behind the bar. Iron Knife started to walk toward the bar.

He stopped, as Horne stood up to full height, leveled the Greener at them.

"Hooough!" yelled Iron Knife and snatched his tomahawk from his belt. The other braves drew knives and 'hawks, began yelling war cries.

Horne ticked off both barrels of the Greener at point blank range. A spray of double ought buck raked the chests of Iron Knife, Crow Caller and Seven Stars, rattled against the adobe walls, the shutters. The men screamed in agony and fell down.

Gray Elk threw his 'hawk straight at Horne. Horne threw the Greener at him, ducked. He picked up the trade musket, trained it on Diving Eagle, who was closest, and pulled the trigger. There was a moment's delay as the fine powder in the frizzen *poufed,* then spread fire through the touchhole. It sounded like a light cough. Then the rifle exploded flame and chunks of German silver. Gray Elk's body spurted blood in a dozen places. One of his eyes blew back in its socket and he writhed like a man being eaten alive by ants as he corkscrewed in a half–circle before he fell. Seven Stars leaped across the bar, grabbed Horne by the throat. He squeezed, and Horne felt the light dim in the room.

The Indian's grip tightened on Horne's windpipe. He felt himself sinking. He struggled for air, but none came in through his mouth. His lungs began to burn as he fought to expel the dead air. His knees buckled and he went down.

From somewhere far away, he heard a woman scream, and then a rifle shot, so muffled, he thought his ears must be stuffed with cotton. He reached a hand out desperately, but the Indian was too far away. His hand fell, touched something hard, closed around it.

"I kill Gray Wolf!" screamed Seven Stars in Arapaho.

Horne felt the man's weight slide over the bar and he knew that he had only seconds of life left.

Seven Stars' face swam above him, then wrinkled into a maddening blur as the darkness closed in on Horne, clotting his senses to a final standstill.

A girl screamed, more shrilly than the other, as Seven Stars fell over the edge of the bar, crashed into Horne's chest.

CHAPTER 16

SEVEN Stars' fall broke his grip on Horne's windpipe. Horne expelled stale air, sucked in a fresh breath. Life returned to his extremities. His vision cleared. The darkness parted, Seven Stars swam back into focus. Horne felt the weight of the wiry brave on his chest, saw Seven Stars claw for his knife.

Horne's fingers squeezed the butt of the Spanish pistol in his hand. Seven Stars reached for Horne's throat again as he brought his blade up over his head. Horne twisted, shoved the pistol into the Arapaho's side. For a moment the two men looked at each other, their blazing eyes locked, warrior to warrior.

Seven Stars grunted, plunged the knife downward. Horne squeezed the trigger. The Spanish pistol bucked in his hand. The knifeblade grazed his cheek, thunked into the dirt floor next to his head. Seven Stars twitched, let out a sigh and fell sideways. Blood from his wound soaked into Horne's buckskin shirt. He crawled out from under the brave, snatched Seven Stars' knife up in his left hand. He drove the blade into the brave's throat. Seven Stars kicked one last time, slumped over in death, filling the air with a foul scent as his sphincter muscle relaxed.

Horne struggled to his feet, put the emptied pistol in his belt. He wiped blood from his hand onto his leggings, picked up the other pistol and his Hawken. He staggered to the door, his throat sore as a bad tooth, his shoulder muscles aching.

He stood there, witness to a scene of horror. Red Hawk stood over Sally May's lifeless body. He had a hank of her hair in his hand. He jerked his arm, and the scalplock made a sound like ripping canvas. He shoved the bloody scalp in his sash, next to another. Horne's glance swept the compound. Betsy June Simmons was dead. She lay sprawled on her back, her dress torn wide open, her throat cut. A patch of hair and scalp were missing from the side of her head.

"Red Hawk," rasped Horne. His glance took in the other girl, Mary Lee, who stood openmouthed by a wagon wheel, her back pressed against it as she stared down at her sister's mutilated skull.

The Arapaho looked at the white man with piercing eyes. Blood flecked his hands and wrists. He took a step backwards, toward Mary Lee.

"Run girl," Horne said in English.

Mary Lee stared at him with shock–widened eyes. She seemed to look right through him. Her face bore no expression. Her lower lip quivered slightly. Unlike her sisters, she wore a doeskin dress, beautifully beaded. An Arapaho shawl draped her slender shoulders. Her hair was braided, and she had vermillion smeared on her cheeks. She looked, Horne thought, like some painted harlot, hideously dressed up like a squaw bride.

"Woman no run," Red Hawk said in English. He glared at Horne in defiance. Then his mouth broke in a grin and he whirled, charged toward Mary Lee with his arm cocked, the bloody scalping knife raised high.

Horne shot him in the back, low, with the Spanish flintlock pistol. The ball smacked against bone, jarred the brave to his knees. Red Hawk twisted, stood up, staggered toward Horne.

Mary Lee screamed as Horne cocked the Hawken's set trigger.

"It is a good day to die," hissed Red Hawk, his hand still gripping the knife. His sash, ripped where the ball had come through, dripped flesh blood.

"About a dozen years too late," said Horne, in English. He

ticked the front trigger of the Hawken. He held the weapon waist high and Red Hawk just walked into the bullet. The ball smashed his breastplate, punched through a lung, cracked two ribs and blew out a chunk of fist–sized flesh and bone as it emerged from his back. He pitched forward, falling headlong at Horne's feet, gurgled once in his throat and went slack.

Mary Lee screamed, and dropped to her knees beside Red Hawk. Gently, she turned him over. Horne reached down and snatched the two scalps from his belt, stuffed them into his possibles pouch.

He looked down at Mary Lee Simmons. Violent sobs wracked her body. Horne shook his head, walked over to the adobe wall, set his rifle against it. He reloaded the Hawken, and his Spanish pistols. He could not stand to look at the grieving girl again. Not yet.

He went inside, found pack saddles, panniers, rope. He unhitched all four mules, put the pack saddles on two of them. He filled the panniers with grain, airtights, salt pork, bacon, coffee, ball and powder. He got these from the goods in the wagons, made sure the weight of the panniers was equal. He threw tarp over the saddles, hitched them in double diamonds. He stripped the Indian ponies, rigged line through their halters.

"Which pony you want to ride?" he asked the girl.

She looked up at him with red–rimmed eyes. Tears streaked her face.

"Who are you?" she asked numbly as she stood up, wrapped her Arapaho shawl around her. The weave and pattern looked familiar to Horne, but he only glanced at it for a moment as his gaze met hers.

"I'm Horne," he said.

"Why did you kill him?" she said huskily, the tears breaking through again.

"He was fixing to kill you, girl."

"No! He wasn't! He wouldn't!"

"Missy, you pick out a pony to ride and pull yourself together."

She rushed toward him, threw herself at him. She pounded on his chest with tiny balled-up fists, screaming hysterically. He grabbed her shoulders and shook her.

"Red Hawk just *murdered* your sisters," he said softly.

Her eyes blazed and narrowed in disbelief—even though she had witnessed this horror for herself. Then she crumpled into a fainting swoon. Horne caught her before she hit the ground, drew her to him. She whimpered against his chest as the hysteria made her muscles twitch involuntarily.

There was more to this than her people would ever understand, Horne knew. She had been with the Arapaho band for more than a year. Much could happen in a woman's heart during that time. He had seen women hostages fall in love with their cruel captors before. He could never understand it, never explain it to himself. He had seen young Indian girls beaten and raped by Arapaho braves. He had seen these same girls look at their men, later, with worshipping eyes, adoring glances.

"Girl?" Horne asked, when she came to.

She looked up at him, her eyes pleading for some release from the pain she felt. Horne felt his insides twist up.

"I *loved* my sisters," she said in a whisper. "I'm heartsick that they died . . . but Red Hawk, he . . ."

"No need to go on about it. You can work and worry the kinks out of that knot in time, child."

"I—I'm not a child. Not anymore."

"Which Simmons girl are you?"

"Mary Lee," she said, and her voice caught in her throat.

"Take a pony and go outside," he said gently. "I'll see to the buryin'. You wait for me. We got a long ride."

For a moment he thought she was going to defy him, but she grabbed up the reins of her pony and led him through the gate. Horne followed, a few minutes later, leading Tony, the mules and Indian ponies. He hitched them along the rail.

"What are you going to do?" Mary Lee asked.

"You just sit tight. I'll be back soon."

He walked back into the compound, methodically took Red Hawk's scalp, then dragged the body into a horse stall. He laid the girls out in another, folding their hands over their abdomens.

He sprinkled coal oil over the bodies of the dead braves, and over every piece of wood in the place until it ran out. He threw the can down, heard its empty clatter. He found a box of sulphur matches and struck them, lighting his fires, one by one, in the post, in the stalls and stables. The fire hissed, black smoke curled upward, wood crackled as it fed on the flames.

He walked outside, unhitched the animals, mounted Tony. Mary Lee was waiting for him, astride a small paint.

"What did you do?" she asked, wrinkling her nose. The smell of burning oil blew towards them.

"Nothing will bother them," he said laconically.

They rode to the south, and every so often Mary Lee looked back over her shoulder at the black column of smoke rising in the sky. Then she would look at Horne, and search his impassive face for some expression that she could understand.

A silence hung between them, and Horne knew that it was the secret they shared about Red Hawk and her. Sometimes her eyes would go cloudy, mist with tears because she was keeping it all inside her like a festering wound that wouldn't heal over. It was sad, too, for both of them, because the secret was so big and so shameful neither of them would talk about it.

But the secret was also a bond between them, a cipher that only they could unravel if they wished.

After they crossed the Platte and neared the foothills, Mary Lee Simmons did not look back anymore at the trading post that blazed with a raging, scourging fire.

CHAPTER 17

IN the long months following Horne's departure from the valley, the villagers wondered what had happened to him. Another September came and went. By November of '53, some thought he was dead, though others were not so sure. The cabins in that broad valley bred their own fevers and the guilt among the men festered. Lou and Elizabeth Simmons took over Caleb's store, and their presence was a constant reminder that none of them had gone off to rescue the Simmons girls. Only the man they all hated had done this. Only the man none of them trusted was tracking the Indians who had murdered Caleb and little Angus.

It was bitter fruit they chewed in Sky Valley, and they fought and argued over their decision long after another winter locked them in tight, deep snows clogging the passes, and long after any hope of Horne's ever returning had vanished.

"Will Horne be back?" asked Lou Simmons bitterly, one day in mid–November.

No one answered.

The snows followed Horne and the girl over the pass, locked them in for the rest of November. Horne saw the blizzard coming, and he made camp by a stream, cut a shelter, shielded it with spruce bows. He and Mary Lee Simmons laid in the firewood wordlessly, built a lean–to for the stock.

The wind whistled down on them, and the snow drifted high, blocking the trail. At night, when they slept, Horne listened to her whimper in her dreams, and each day he avoided looking at the dullness in her eyes, the tremor of her lower lip. At night, when the fire burned high, they sat and sipped coffee and listened to the relentless howling of the wind.

When the storm broke, the cougars came.

Horne squatted at the stream, filling an empty peach tin with water for the horses and mules. He heard the high–pitched bray of the mules, the shriek of the horses. Then Mary Lee screamed.

Horne picked up the Hawken at his side, slipped the buckskin sheath from it, let it fall to the snow. He headed for camp at a run. A cougar embraced a pony's back, raked its hide with sharp talons. The pony squealed in terror. Horne set the hair trigger on his Hawken, took aim and fired. The cougar snarled, coughed in pain and twisted off the pony's back.

Horne drew his knife, raced to the fallen cougar, prepared to cut its throat. It writhed, roiling the snow, spattering its blood in every direction. Mary Lee screamed again, and he turned, saw her running toward him, another cougar padding behind her, closing the gap in long, graceful leaps. Its black–tipped tail twitched.

"Help me, Horne!" she screamed.

Horne ran to her, threw her down in the snow. The cougar leaped into the air. Horne caught the animal, full brunt, went down in a tangle of claws and teeth and tawny hide. He felt his buckskins rip as the cat dug in its hind paws, trying to disembowel him. He felt its hot breath on his face, the fetid stink of its teeth.

Horne sank the knife into the cougar's back, felt it rasp on bone. He stabbed it again, rolled to get it off him, but the enraged puma stuck to him, trying to bite through his neck. Horne brought a knee up hard into the cat's belly, struck at its throat with the blade of his knife. Again and again, he buried the knife to the hilt in soft fur and flesh. The animal choked, coughed and slid away, mortally wounded. Horne rose up to his knees, groggy, and plunged the knife into the cougar's heart, twisted until the blood stopped pumping. He crawled away on his hands and knees, fell atop Mary Lee, gasping for breath.

"Are you—are you—all right?" he stammered.

"Uh huh," she murmured. He panted as he pushed away from her.

"Stay here," he said. He stood up, lurched toward the other cougar. The mules were kicking it, although it was already dead. The animal sounds of terror were a cacophony in Horne's ears. He shoved the mules away, dragged the cougar off where the horses and mules couldn't see it. Soon, they quieted down as he began to skin the first cougar.

Mary Lee rubbed salve on Horne's scratches that night. He sewed up his own shirt. Neither ate very much, but they sat closer together at the fire.

"Horne, I don't know how to face them," she said.

"Who?"

"Ma and pa. The others."

"You face them, that's all."

"What do I tell them? How can I explain what happened?"

"You don't, if you can't."

"But, they'll want to know."

She wrapped her shawl around her head. It was quiet with the wind down, and for the first time in weeks no snow was falling. The cougar hides lay spread out atop their shelter, keeping the warmth of the fire inside. Horne looked up from his sewing, set the awl down by the fire.

"No one can know what's in your heart, Mary Lee. Some things you keep inside, and they hurt. But you don't tell your folks anything. Nor anyone else."

"You make it out to be easy," she said, almost pouting.

"Ain't easy. But, I know how you feel."

"Oh, what would you know about how I feel?"

He sighed, looked at her eyes. The dullness was gone. Firelight flickered in their depths. Maybe her brush with death had brought her back to life, he mused. Maybe she would come out of her shell.

"That shawl you're wearin'," he said softly. "Red Hawk give it to you?"

"Yes."

"Know where he got it?"

"He—he carried it around with him. It was some kind of medicine shawl."

"It belonged to my wife," said Horne.

"Your wife? I didn't know . . . you mean . . . an Indian squaw?"

"Not a squaw. A woman. She was Cheyenne."

There was a stretch of silence between them.

"What happened to her?"

"She's dead. Red Hawk sold her for whiskey when he was through with her."

"I don't believe you," she snapped.

Horne picked up the awl again. He dug at the garment, ran the sinew through and pulled the loop tight. A muscle in his jaw twitched.

"What—what was her name?" Mary Lee stuttered.

"Sleeping Water. She was very beautiful."

"You—you loved her?"

"I did, I reckon. She was some woman."

Mary Lee didn't say anything for several moments. She just stared at Horne as if seeing him for the first time.

"I believe you," she said. "I'm sorry."

"It happened a long time ago," he said.

"You must have hated Red Hawk a lot."

Horne tied the last stitch in his shirt, put the awl back in his saddlebag.

"Once, we were friends," he said softly. "I didn't hate him. The white man gave him the burning cup. He just wasn't strong enough to push it away."

"Yes," said Mary Lee thoughtfully, "I know."

A look passed between them, for an instant, then they both

looked away. They stared into the fire as it burned low and the darkness moved in close. Their faces reflected the glowing light, became like hammered bronze masks behind which their emotions boiled and simmered, hidden from sight in the glittering depths of their eyes.

In late December, Horne and Mary Lee rode into the valley. Tony had broken one of his legs and Horne had had to shoot him. He now rode the steeldust gray that had been Iron Knife's pony. Horne had shaved six days ago, but now his face was grizzled. They had left the other ponies and the mules at the top of the ridge. Horne would come back for them later.

Mary Lee started sniffling as soon as they saw the smoke spiraling from her chimney, from McGonigle's store.

"Horne, please," she said. "I—I don't want to go back there. I—I can't."

"You hush up, Mary Lee," he gruffed. "You got to go back. Some things you just gotta face."

"I—I can't face them alone."

The gray trotted away from her, then, and he gave the animal its head.

The people of the Valley gathered in front of McGonigle's. They stood, silent as wraiths, as the first flakes of snow danced down, swirled around their faces. Horne halted the gray in front of them, waited for Mary Lee to ride up. She stopped her pony beside his, and looked at the assemblage.

Elizabeth Simmons rushed up to them, skirts flying. She looked at her daughter in horror. Lou Simmons hobbled closer, licked dry lips.

"Here's your daughter, ma'am," said Horne.

"My child," Elizabeth murmured, "what have they done to you? What did *he* do to you?"

"Oh, ma, I—I can't tell you. Please don't ask me any questions."

Horne swung out of the saddle. He wore one of the

Spanish pistols on his belt. He walked toward Luke Newcastle, who stepped out of the crowd to meet him.

"Your brother tried to kill me, Luke," said Horne.

"Too bad he didn't."

Puzzled looks wrinkled the faces of the men and women gathered there.

"Did you get them Injuns," demanded MacPherson. "Did you avenge my boy's death?"

Newcastle had a pistol in his belt. He didn't take his eyes off Horne.

"They're all dead," said Horne. "Hardy Newcastle, too. Luke, here, told the Arapaho about this valley. They knew you were down here. They knew about the Simmons girls."

Jules Moreaux looked at Horne with glittering eyes. Jacques Berthoud sucked in a breath. Faron MacGregor opened his mouth to say something. Berle Campbell exchanged a bewildered glance with Chollie Winder. Chollie's son Gary swallowed as his eyes widened.

Luke Newcastle clawed for his pistol. The settlers backed away from him.

"Horne, look out!" cried Mary Lee. Her parents turned around, saw the two men squaring off.

Luke drew his pistol, but he was slow, nervous. He spilled powder, trying to cock the hammer on the flintlock.

Horne drew the Spanish pistol, cocked it, and fired. Luke staggered backwards, a hole in his belly. Blood blossomed on his coat.

"He was the cause of your trouble," said Horne. "Intentional or not."

"You murdered that man in cold blood," shrieked Elizabeth Simmons. "What have you done with Betsy June and Sally May, you beast?"

"Ma!" shouted Mary Lee. "He tried to save them. He saved me!"

"I reckon I killed Luke there, same as his brother," said Horne, looking each man in the eye as he spoke. "I would have given him no more than a good horsewhipping and let him live out his days sufferin' for what he did."

"Aye, mon, you did what you had to," said MacGregor, breaking the silence. "We'll digest it as we can. Newcastle drew first."

"So did his brother," said Horne.

He climbed back on his horse, slipped the red–haired scalplocks from the rigging. He handed them to Lou Simmons. "You might want to keep these to remember your girls by," he said.

The two Frenchmen crossed themselves as Horne rode off toward his own cabin. Elizabeth stretched her arms out, tried to drag Mary Lee from the saddle.

Mary Lee drew back, slapped her reins against the pony's sides. She rode after Horne. "Horne!" she called. "Wait for me."

Horne did not turn around.

She caught up to him, rode alongside, panting for breath. "Horne, take me with you. I—I can't face them. I knew I couldn't."

"You didn't try."

"I want to be your squaw—your woman, I mean."

"Well, I got to think about that."

"But you know about me. You know and you don't hold it against me like they will. And, I go weak every time I think about that mountain lion, how close he came to . . . You don't hate me, do you? Like they do?"

"No. They don't hate you, either."

"But they—I saw the way they all looked at me. I saw the disgust in their faces."

"Maybe right off, they did. You got to give them a chance."

"Will you give me a chance?" She seemed on the verge of weeping.

He looked at her. There was no pity in his look. There was nothing in his eyes, either, to tell her what he was thinking just then.

"You can come along," he said. "I reckon you might want to get your thoughts gathered up some before you go back."

"Yes," she said eagerly. She fell silent as they rode into the trees, left the settlement behind.

"I told you what would happen," said Bill MacPherson.

"Yep, that mountain man done sullied your only live daughter," agreed Merle Campbell.

"Get her back, Louis," snapped Elizabeth.

"I don't want her back," her husband replied, staring at nothing on the distant ridge. He brought his gaze down to the locks of hair in his hand. He stretched his fingers out slowly. The scalplocks dropped from his hand, floated to the ground. "I don't ever want to hear her name mentioned again."

"She's our daughter," wailed Elizabeth.

"No, not any more," said Lou, and the silence grew as the snowfall thickened, blurred the faces of the people standing in a helpless semicircle around Luke Newcastle's body. It was as though they were in a cemetery, where a grave was slowly filling up without a single human hand touching shovel or spade.